PIGS MIGHT FLY

He looked up into the sky again and tried to imagine him-self up there, legs beating away, ears flapping, curly tail stretched out straight behind him as he soared and glided and swooped.

Perhaps if I got up somewhere high, he thought, so that I could jump off and then start flying . . . I'm sure I could do it. I will do it—you see if I don't. Just give me half a chance.

"A book as fresh as the very speculation that pigs might fly."
—*Horn Book*

Pigs Might Fly

Pigs Might Fly

A novel by Dick King-Smith

Drawings by Mary Rayner

PUFFIN BOOKS

PUFFIN BOOKS
Published by the Penguin Group
Viking Penguin, a division of Penguin Books USA Inc.,
375 Hudson Street, New York, New York 10014, U.S.A.
Penguin Books Ltd, 27 Wrights Lane, London W8 5TZ, England
Penguin Books Australia Ltd, Ringwood, Victoria, Australia
Penguin Books Canada Ltd, 10 Alcorn Avenue, Toronto, Ontario, Canada M4V 3B2
Penguin Books (N.Z.) Ltd, 182–190 Wairau Road, Auckland 10, New Zealand

Penguin Books Ltd, Registered Offices: Harmondsworth, Middlesex, England

First published in Great Britain as *Daggie Dogfoot* by Victor Gollancz Ltd 1980
First published in the United States of America by The Viking Press 1982
Published in Puffin Books 1990
3 5 7 9 10 8 6 4
Text copyright © Dick King-Smith, 1980
Illustrations copyright © Mary Rayner, 1980
Copyright © Viking Penguin Inc., 1982
All rights reserved

LIBRARY OF CONGRESS CATALOGING IN PUBLICATION DATA
King-Smith, Dick.   [Daggie Dogfoot]
Pigs might fly / by Dick King-Smith ; illustrated by Mary Rayner.   p.   cm.
London ed. published as: Daggie Dogfoot. 1980.
Summary: Having been coached in swimming by a duck and an otter, a
runt piglet with deformed front feet becomes a hero when their farm
is flooded.
ISBN 0-14-034537-X
[1. Pigs—Fiction. 2. Farm life—Fiction. 3. Physically
handicapped—Fiction. 4. England—Fiction.] I. Rayner, Mary, ill.
II. Title.
PZ7.K5893Pi 1990   [Fic]—dc20   90-32843

Printed in the United States of America
Set in Aster

CONTENTS

1. TAKEN AWAY *3*
2. NOT IT BUT HE *10*
3. PIGS MIGHT FLY *20*
4. THE SQUIRE *27*
5. RESTHAVEN *37*
6. FELICITY *44*
7. GOSH! *51*
8. THE TRUTH COMES OUT *59*
9. THE RACE *68*
10. IZAAK *75*
11. THE FLOOD *86*
12. GOING FOR HELP *96*
13. MAN ON A RAFT *105*
14. ON THE DAM *112*
15. BREAKFAST AND BED *120*
16. DREAMS *127*

Contents

17. THE BIG STRANGE BIRD *131*
18. MISSING *136*
19. AN AWFUL SHOCK *142*
20. "NOT MIGHT, BUT CAN!" *147*
21. HOME AND DRY *153*

Pigs Might Fly

Taken Away

"Oh, no!" cried Mrs. Barleylove miserably. "Oh, no!"

"What is it, dear?" came the voice of Mrs. Gobble-spud next door. "One dead?"

"No," said Mrs. Barleylove. "Not yet anyway."

Mrs. Barleylove was a pedigree Gloucester Old Spots, a flop-eared white pig spotted with black blobs of color, as though a giant had flicked his paintbrush at her. During the night she had given birth to eight babies, seven of them all of a size, round and strong-looking and already plumped out with their first milk. But the eighth, she now saw, was a poor spindly little creature, half as big as the rest, with a head too large for its scrawny body and a look of hopelessness on its face.

It was a runt, a piglet born for some reason far smaller and weaker than its brothers and sisters. In different parts of England they are called by different names—cads, wasters, or nesslegraffs. In Gloustershire they call them dags.

There was a rustling and a scrabbling in the next sty, and Mrs. Gobblespud's head appeared over the wall.

"Oh, dear me," she said. "Oh, dear me, Mrs. B. Oh, I am sorry. It isn't just a smallish one, is it?"

"No," said Mrs. Barleylove. "It's a real dag."

Most of the Old Spots sows in the range of nine sties had probably had a dag at some time in their careers as mothers. It wasn't thought of as a disgrace, something to be whispered about, because it didn't seem to be anyone's fault. But it was thought to be a pity, a great pity, for every sow's ambition was to rear a fine litter of healthy, evenly matched youngsters, and as the news spread that morning, there was much worried grunting and rolling of eyes and shaking of long, droopy ears.

The servant wouldn't like it either, they said to each other. They thought of the Pigman as a servant since he did nothing but minister to their wants; he fed them, he watered them, he cleaned them out and brought them fresh bedding. They spoke of him

—and to him, though he could not understand this—simply as "Pigman," as a Roman nobleman might have said "Slave." Pigman wouldn't be pleased about Mrs. Barleylove's dag, for dags, if they survived, grew very, very slowly and were more trouble than they were worth.

Mrs. Barleylove's neighbor on the other side was called Mrs. Swiller, and she was leaning over her wall, gossiping with the next lady down the line, Mrs. Swedechopper.

"It's not just that it's a dag, Mrs. Swedechopper," she said sadly. "From what I can see of the poor little soul, it's deformed."

"Deformed, Mrs. Swiller?" said Mrs. Swedechopper in a tone of horror. "Why, what do you mean?"

"Well, its front feet aren't right."

"Not right?"

"No. They turn inward. And they don't look like pig's trotters. More like dog's feet."

Mrs. Gobblespud, too, had noticed this further piece of misfortune for poor Mrs. Barleylove and had told her neighbor, Mrs. Maizemunch, and everywhere heads were sticking up as the sows rested their forefeet comfortably on their boundary walls and discussed the situation. Only at Number Five, in the center of the row of sties, was no head raised, for Mrs. Barleylove still stood sadly contemplating her misshapen child, while its seven brothers and sisters squeaked greedily around her legs, begging her to lie down and give them more milk. When she did so, the dag was knocked down in the general rush and lay for a moment upside down in the straw, his curious clubfeet waving helplessly.

Even when he righted himself and tried to feed, he was continually pushed aside by the others and got very little. From Mrs. Troughlicker at Number One to Mrs. Grubguzzle at Number Nine, everybody was convinced of one thing. Pigman would never let this one stay.

"Pigman'll take him," they said.

"No doubt about it."

"Stands to reason—with feet like that."

"Poor little thing."

"Pigman'll take him away for sure." And gloom hung over the pigsties like a black cloud.

The sows never quite knew what happened to a dag or, for that matter, a piglet badly hurt by being stepped or lain on by its mother. They knew that the servant came and removed such an unfortunate, so they simply spoke of it as being "taken away"; they were unaware of the hardwood club the pigman kept in his shed to deal out merciful death to the weak and the wounded.

Before long, the distant clank of buckets and good smells blowing on the wind told them that the servant was bringing breakfast. The low grunts of

concern changed to loud, impatient yells as the dag
was forgotten in the excitement of feeding time.

"Hurry up, Pigman!" shouted the sows.

"Stir your stumps, you lazy thing!"

"He's too slow to catch a cold!"

And Mrs. Troughlicker at Number One, who
would be the first fed, champed her jaws with a

noise like clapping hands, and great dribbles of spit ran out of her mouth.

When the Pigman had completed his duties and Mrs. Grubguzzle's head was deep in the trough at Number Nine, he returned to Mrs. Barleylove. Earlier that morning he had seen that the birth was finished and all seemed well, but he had not yet examined the litter. Of course, he immediately saw the dag and gently and without hesitation picked it up and popped it into the deep pocket of his old apron, unnoticed by the sow busy at her breakfast. If he had wanted to examine or remove a healthy piglet, he would have clamped its mouth shut to prevent its squeals bringing the mother rushing to its defense, but this one, he thought, didn't have the strength for even a squeak.

In the shed he looked at it more closely. In all his long experience he had never seen a piglet with such funny forefeet. The little points of the tiny hooves were turned inward toward one another, so that the shape of the foot was not sharp but rounded, as Mrs. Swiller had said, like a puppy's.

Now Gloucester Old Spots are a rare breed of pig, and the Pigman occasionally gave in to the temptation to spare the life of a dag if it was a female. A little sow piglet, or "hilt" as he called it, just might grow, even if very slowly, to make a breeding sow one day. But little boar piglets, called hogs, he wanted nothing to do with if they were born weak.

Not only was this one a hog, it also had those awful feet. Hanging on a rusty nail was his hard-wood club, and the Pigman reached for it.

2

Not IT, but HE

Strangely enough, people who keep pigs very often seem to look like them. The Pigman was a huge fat person, with short legs and a big stomach. His face had several chins, a squashed nose, and little dark glinty eyes. He also had enormous hands, and in one of these he held the dag as one might hold a bunch of flowers, its bony sad-looking head and curious fore-feet sticking out above his curled fingers. He shifted his grasp to hold the creature by its hind legs, its head now hanging down, and took a good grip on his club with the other hand. At that very moment he heard a scuttling noise at the other end of the shed, and, turning, he saw a rat running across the top of one of his meal bins.

Now if there was one thing the Pigman hated, it was a rat. Rats, as far as he was concerned, were worthless, greedy, cunning thieves, plotting from dawn to dusk to steal the food of his beloved pigs, and the sight of a rat was enough to make him forget everything else. He dropped the dag headfirst on the floor and lumbered toward the meal bin, grunting with fury.

The first thing the dag saw, when he had picked himself up, was bright sunlight outside the door, and he tottered toward it and fell down the concrete steps into the yard. Once outside, he heard in the distance the contented noises of full-fed sows and the squeals of piglets fighting for a place at the milk bar, and he turned that way. He was weak and confused and hungry and unhappy. But he was also determined and wanted his mother and was going to find her even if, as seemed likely, it killed him.

He plodded on on his dog feet and eventually reached the door of Number One, where he had just enough strength left for some feeble squeaking. Mrs. Troughlicker's head appeared over the door.

"Upon my soul!" she cried. "It's that little dag that Pigman took away! Mrs. Barleylove! Mrs. Barleylove! It's your dag! It's little Daggie Dogfoot!"

There was an uproar along the row as every sow lurched to her feet, those with piglets shaking them off and scattering them in screaming confusion. Soon on every front door there rested a pair of trotters, and above each a large drop-eared face gazed down at the object outside Mrs. Troughlicker's sty.

Above the hubbub came the deep urgent grunting of little Daggie Dogfoot's mother at Number Five. When Mrs. Barleylove had finished breakfast, she had nosed her newborn litter and, though she could not count, had found them all fat and level and had known that Pigman had taken one away. Now, by some miracle, here he was again, not a dozen yards from home.

"Daggie!" she called. "Daggie! Come on, son! Don't give up now."

Slowly the exhausted baby began to cover the last lap, wobbling along past Mrs. Boltapple at Number

Two, then Mrs. Swedechopper, then Mrs. Swiller, till at last he stood swaying with weariness at the door of Number Five.

"Mommy," said Daggie Dogfoot, "I'm tired. And I'm hungry. Let me in."

Mrs. Barleylove would have broken down the door without a second thought if she had been able to, but it was strong and opened inward. Rooting frantically at the bottom of it in a vain attempt to lift it off its hinges, she discovered that there was a narrow gap between its lower edge and the concrete, a gap not wide enough to get her snout through or to allow a fat piglet out, but just sufficient perhaps to let a very thin piglet in. She scraped away all the straw from it and snorted madly under it as though she were trying to sniff Daggie in like a vacuum cleaner.

"Come on, baby," she said. "Just get your head through, and the rest'll come easy."

"Go on, little one!" shouted Mrs. Grubguzzle at Number Nine, and she was echoed by Mrs. Grazegrass, Mrs. Maizemunch, and Mrs. Gobblespud, as well as by the ladies whose doors Daggie had already passed.

"Go on, baby!" they shouted. "We're all behind you!"

And through the combination of their support and his mother's urging and his own determination, with a last desperate effort Daggie Dogfoot somehow squeezed his head beneath the door and scrabbled with his funny forefeet and pushed with his skinny hind legs and found himself at last back home. He lay exhausted while with tender grunts his mother carefully licked him all over. All down the line there rose a chorus of snorts of relief, and Mrs. Swiller and Mrs. Gobblespud got off their doors and up on their boundary walls for final words of congratulation.

"I love it!" cried Mrs. Gobblespud. "What a brave little pig it is!"

Mrs. Barleylove looked up from her licking.

"Begging your pardon, Mrs. Gobblespud," she said slowly and severely, "it isn't an 'it.' He's a 'he.'"

"She's right," said Mrs. Swiller. "And not just a 'he.' I reckon he's a hero." And with a few last good wishes both ladies returned to their duties.

Fortunately, by the time Daggie had made his way back to the pigsties, his mother had not only finished her own breakfast but had also given his brothers and sisters theirs. So now she was able to push and prod and nose their well-fed little bodies into the inner covered part of Number Five, to barricade the opening with her great spotted back, and to offer the whole range of the milk bar to one thin, tired little body.

And how he drank! Moving along the line, scrabbling at his mother's side with his puppy's feet, he drank and drank and drank. And as he drank, color seemed to come into his skin, and his tummy blew out like a drum, and some sparkle crept into his dull eyes. Ten minutes later, when the Pigman looked over the door, he found it hard to recognize his late intended victim.

The Pigman's pursuit of the rat had led to much moving of bins and sacks, which in turn had exposed other rats. And from this followed much swearing and heavy breathing and wild swiping with the hardwood club, and cries of "Dratyer!" and "Dangyer!" and "Blastyer!" At the end of it all he was hot and sweaty, and the rats were laughing in their runways, and quite a lot of time had passed.

He looked around the doorway end of the shed, expecting to find the dag hiding somewhere, then searched the yard, and finally, seeing no sign of him, walked down to the sties in case the piglet could by any chance have found his way home. He leaned on the door of Number Five and shook his head till his three chins wobbled.

"I'd never have believed it," he said to himself, mopping his face with a red spotted handkerchief. "That kid's got some guts. But all the same he'll never be no use to no one, nohow. He'll have to go." And he slid back the bolt.

Now Mrs. Barleylove, busy at breakfast and un-aware of the fact—though resigned to the possibility—that one of her children was to be taken away, was one thing. Mrs. Barleylove interrupted while feeding that hero of a child was another.

Heaving herself to her feet with a violence that threw a surprised Daggie far to one side, she ran at the servant, swinging her head and champing her jaws together so that a froth of bubbles ran out over her tusks. The chomping and her furious grunting combined to make a noise that sounded to the Pigman like "Out! Out! Out!" which, in fact, was exactly what she was saying. At the same time, Mrs.

Swiller and Mrs. Gobblespud reared onto their walls and also shouted angrily at the servant.

"You leave him alone, Pigman!" they roared.

"Poor little fellow!"

"Tackle somebody your own size!"

"Dirty fat man!"

For just as we say "dirty as a pig" or "fat as a pig," so pigs repay the insult the other way around. And all along the row, from Mrs. Troughlicker to Mrs. Grubguzzle, the cry went up, "Dirty fat man! Leave him alone!" while nine pairs of jaws champed and nine pairs of eyes glittered.

The Pigman got out of Number Five remarkably quickly for a man of his size. He knew all about the damage an angry sow can cause, and it was a different kind of sweat that he now wiped from his brow.

"Dratyer!" the Pigman cried, and "Dangyer!" and "Blastyer!"

He waited until the fuming Mrs. Barleylove had gotten off the top of her door, and then he bolted it and lumbered off, grumbling to himself. Let her keep the horrible little dag, he thought, it'll die soon enough and save me the trouble. Blasted old sows!

And as men often do when they feel that women-folk are too much for them, he walked across the yard to seek the company of another male, for the Gloucester Old Spots boar lived opposite. The boar came to his door and gave his usual order.

"Hey, you, Pigman. Scratch my back." And the servant, of course, obeyed. He's not a bad guy really, thought the boar. Does what he's told.

He's a good old guy, thought the Pigman. "Aren't you, old man?" he said. "Not like those nasty old sows."

And indeed, except that one was spotted and one was not, they looked very much alike as they stood and chatted, each in his own tongue.

3

Pigs Might Fly

Time passed, and Daggie Dogfoot not only survived but grew. He did not expand visibly like his litter mates, but by cunning and agility he secured a fair share of his mother's milk. For example, he would persuade her to lie across a corner in which he was already waiting, or stand alongside the concrete feeding trough so that he could scramble onto its rim for a high-level drink which the others couldn't reach; their slippery sharp-hooved forefeet did not allow them to balance there.

The Pigman became resigned to Daggie's survival, and persuaded himself he had kept the creature out of kindness, as a mascot. Well aware of the look in

Mrs. Barleylove's eye and the sound of her threatening grunts, he left the dag severely alone.

Mrs. Barleylove's neighbors spent a lot of their spare time leaning over their respective walls to watch. Unlike the Pigman, who was merely pretending, they really did regard Daggie as a mascot, as did all the other mothers; no piglet had ever before been "taken away" and then come back, and there seemed something magical, almost mystical, about this, and also about his feet, which appeared at the moment to be an advantage to him rather than the reverse.

"I love him!" said Mrs. Gobblespud one morning after watching Daggie do his King-of-the-Castle trick on the trough. "He's smart, isn't he, Mrs. B.?"

Mrs. Barleylove only grunted, but inwardly she swelled with pride. She had never believed in having favorites among her many children, but she had to admit to herself that this one was special.

"No offense," said Mrs. Swiller, "but his little feet have changed, haven't they?" And indeed, though the hooves on Daggie's hind feet remained normal, the grotesquely inward-curving horny parts on his front feet had fallen off, leaving even more puppy-like round pads. This seemed to make him more surefooted, so that when the litter played a game of tag, racing around the smooth, clean-washed concrete of the outer enclosure after Pigman had mucked out, it was always Daggie who stayed on his feet, while his stronger brothers and sisters often slipped and skidded onto their sides.

Mrs. Barleylove had half a mind to take offense at such a personal remark, but she quickly realized that it was well-meant, and anyway she wanted her neighbors' opinions.

"Yes, they have changed," she said. "To tell you the truth, ladies, I'd be glad to know what you think. You may think I'm crazy, but I've caught myself wondering if he isn't somehow"—she paused and looked around to make sure that Daggie was not listening. He had run off with the rest to roughhouse in the straw inside, so she went on—"somehow . . . special?"

"Special?" said Mrs. Swiller.

"Well, born for some purpose."

"Purpose?" said Mrs. Gobblespud.

"What I mean is," said Mrs. Barleylove, "he was taken away, wasn't he?"

"Musta been," they said.

"And yet he came back?"

"For sure," they said.

"So that's kind of . . . special?"

Long droopy ears slap-slapped against fat faces as the two ladies nodded vigorous agreement.

"And his front feet?" said Mrs. Barleylove.

"Different," said Mrs. Swiller.

"Curious," said Mrs. Gobblespud.

"Special?" asked Mrs. Barleylove.

There was a pause.

"Do you mean," said her neighbors, "special feet . . . for some purpose?"

It was Mrs. Barleylove's turn to nod. There was another pause, during which the neighbors glanced a little anxiously at each other over her head. It occurred to them simultaneously that this was going a bit too far. Mrs. Barleylove's concern for her dag was leading her to flights of fancy. Special feet for some purpose? No, no, that was too much of a good thing.

"Well . . . no, dear, not really," said Mrs. Gobblespud in a kindly voice, "I mean, I know they're not like other piglets' front feet, but . . ."

"What Mrs. G. means, dear," said Mrs. Swiller soothingly, "is that you shouldn't worry about the little fellow's feet. I mean I don't personally think they're going to be a hindrance to him, but as for havir.g been made like that for some purpose—well, that's about as likely as that . . ."

". . . pigs might fly," finished Mrs. Gobblespud.

As Mrs. Swiller had hesitated, Daggie Dogfoot had been on the point of coming out from the inner part of the sty, impelled as children often are by the certain feeling that adults are talking about them. All he heard in fact were the three last words. What's more, his mother and her friends fell silent the moment they saw him, so he was sure he had been right.

"Good morning, Auntie Swiller, good morning, Auntie Gobblespud," he said politely. And then, "Can I have a milk shake, please, Mommy—quick, before the others come back?"

The sows' conversation thus abruptly terminated, the neighbors dropped back off their walls, and Mrs. Barleylove lay down hastily, anxious to please her darling.

Even as he gulped down milk, Daggie was thinking hard. Pigs might fly, he thought, and they were definitely talking about me; that must mean *I* might fly. The other piglets came dashing out at that moment and scrambled and shoved and stamped all over him, but he hung on determinedly until he was finished, and then climbed up and lay down on the huge rubbery cushion of his mother's side.

He looked at his curious feet, about which the others had already begun to tease him, though he did not mind, for he was glad to be alive. He looked up at the blue sky. A sparrow flew over the sty with a whir of wings; a little higher, a flock of starlings made their way across the yard; higher still, the swallows cut lovely circles in the air, and above them all, so high that his baby eyes could hardly see them, the swifts raced, black and crescent-shaped,

screaming their joy at the wonder of flight.

I . . . might fly, thought Daggie Dogfoot. He sat up on his mother and beat his forelegs together experimentally, but nothing happened. Perhaps it's taking off that's difficult, he thought. Perhaps once you get up there, it's easier. He looked up into the sky again and tried to imagine himself up there, legs beating away somehow or other, ears flapping, curly tail stretched out straight behind him as he soared and glided and swooped.

Perhaps if I got up somewhere high, he thought, so that I could jump off and then start flying. I'm sure they were talking about me. I'm sure I could do it. I will do it—you see if I don't. Just give me half a chance.

The Squire

The boar was, of course, the most important person around, partly because he was an incredibly well-bred and aristocratic Gloucester Old Spots, and partly because he was the father of all the children born. His real name was Champion Imperial Challenger III of Ploughbarrow, but the sows all knew him as the Squire. His sty, which was opposite the row of nine, had a sloping veranda-type roof to keep the rain off his noble back, and the Pigman, being large, had to duck under this whenever he went in; the sows appreciated the fact that the servant always bowed low before the master.

The Squire kept in touch with his wives by means

of occasional conversations across the yard when he felt like it and the wind was not too strong. He would stand against his door and poke his head out under his veranda roof and shout at them in his

bluff, jolly way. Sometimes he would address them
generally, and then everyone who was not actually
engaged at that moment in feeding babies would
come respectfully to their front doors and bob their

heads up and down deferentially. Sometimes he would single out an individual.

One morning some weeks after Daggie Dogfoot's birth, the Squire's deep coughing grunt was heard, and the rattle of his door as he heaved his bulk up onto it.

"It's the Squire!" they all said to their neighbors, and waited in awestruck silence. The boar cleared his throat.

"Ah, hhhrm, Mrs. Barleylove, dear lady. A word with you."

"Here I am, Squire," said Mrs. Barleylove.

"The latest children, my dear. I hear from sparrow talk that you have a litter?" The sparrows carried all the gossip around the farm.

"Y-yes, Squire."

"All well, I trust? Chips off the old block?" There was a moment's pause, and a shudder of anticipation ran down the row of sties. But Mrs. Barleylove was equal to the occasion.

"All well, I thank you, Squire," she replied, with hardly a tremor in her voice.

"Good," said the Squire. "Keep up the good work." He got down off his door, while all the ladies ducked their heads again and disappeared with a whistling sound, which was made up of eight small sighs of relief and one large one.

It was not that the Squire didn't know about dags. He knew only too well, because a litter sister of his had been one. He had never forgotten waking up one morning when he was a baby, to find the poor spindly little thing stretched out cold and lifeless beside him, and because of this he was always terrified that one of his own children might be born a dag.

So he always asked the same question, "Chips off the old block?" and the sows never let him down. He never knew that occasionally the chips were very small and either died or were taken away, and as for the occasional hilt whose life the Pigman saw fit to spare, the Squire would not set eyes on it until it was weaned and on its way to other quarters. If it survived that long, it would have caught up a bit in size and be nothing worse than the smallest of the litter. But what on earth would he say about Daggie Dogfoot?

Mrs. Barleylove's neighbors tried to find a tactful way to approach the subject. They began with praise.

"Isn't he active?" said Mrs. Gobblespud admiringly as she watched Daggie, his mind on flight, leap from his mother's back and land upside down in the remains of breakfast at the bottom of the trough. "You must be proud of him, Mrs. B."

"Any mother would be proud of him," said Mrs. Swiller. And then, greatly daring, she added defiantly, "And any father, too."

There was a long, awkward pause, and it seemed to the neighbors that Mrs. Barleylove's white parts grew a little pink and her spots turned slightly blacker.

"I don't know what to do, ladies," she said at last. "Squire's bound to set eyes on him sooner or later. He'll go raving mad."

"It'll be sooner than later though, won't it?" said Mrs. Gobblespud. "They'll be crossing the yard in a week or so, won't they?"

"Crossing the yard" meant weaning time, when the eight-week-old piglets left their mothers and went to the store pens on either side of the boar's sty. Later the hogs would go to the fattening pens, and the hilts to other quarters till they were big enough to be sold for breeding.

Daggie, though he had not been listening closely to the conversation, had, like children everywhere, picked up the awkward bits.

"Who's Squire, Mommy?" he asked.

"The Squire is your father, dear, a very fine gentleman."

"Why will he go raving mad?"

"Oh, your father's a hot-tempered person," said

Mrs. Swiller quickly. "He gets very angry with the servant if his meals are late."

"Well, what does crossing the yard mean, Auntie Swiller?"

"Oh, you'll like that, Daggie," put in Mrs. Gobble-spud soothingly. "That's when all you young ones go off on a lovely vacation and your mother gets a nice rest."

Mrs. Barleylove's other seven piglets jumped up excitedly at this and ran around the sty, squealing, "A lovely vacation! A lovely vacation!" But Daggie Dogfoot sat on his thin backside, and a tear ran down one side of his big head.

"I don't want to leave my mommy," he said, and another tear ran down the other side.

At that moment Mrs. Barleylove made up her mind, quite firmly, that she would not allow this humble, undersized deformed child of hers to cross the yard. Always before, like all the other mothers, she had allowed the servant to drive the weaners away without protest, indeed with a sigh of relief after two months' hard work. This time it would be different, for this child was different, and her heart ached at the sight of those two great tears. The servant could take the other seven, but not her Daggie. Just let him try!

Two weeks later he tried. He opened the door of

Number Five and, holding a sheet of corrugated iron in front of him like a shield, he shooed Mrs. Barleylove into the inner part of the sty while the litter ran out into the yard. A grunt and a rattle on the other side told everyone that the Squire was at his door to inspect his offspring as they crossed. But when the Pigman had shut up Number Five again, he could count only seven fat weaners frisking about outside. He looked back in and saw the dag peeping out from between his mother's legs. He started to open the door again, but immediately Mrs. Barleylove rushed forward, champing and snorting, as fierce as one of her wild woodland ancestors.

"Dirty fat man!" she shouted. "Leave him alone!"

"Dratyer!" cried the Pigman, and "Dangyer!" and "Blastyer!"

But he backed away quickly, and then turned and lumbered off after the rest.

"Keep the miserable thing then!" he shouted back over his shoulder. "It'll never be no use to no one, nohow!"

He rounded up the others, drove them into a V-shaped funnel of hurdles he had put up, then into one of the store pens, and shut them in. He mopped his face with his red spotted handkerchief and went to talk to Champion Imperial Challenger III of Ploughbarrow.

"Hey, you, Pigman. Scratch my back," said the Squire. And, as usual, the servant obeyed. They held a conversation, and it was fortunate that they spoke different languages.

"Fine bunch of youngsters, Pigman," said the Squire. "Fat as you are by the time they're grown, I bet."

"You've got a horrible little dag left over there, old man," said the Pigman. "That bad-tempered old sow's welcome to him."

And what a welcome Daggie Dogfoot was having, for his mother still had plenty of milk left for one, and now the whole milk bar was his and his alone.

At last, full to the brim, he fell asleep by his mother's side, and dreamed that he and she and his father the Squire were all flying, trotter in trotter, through a warm and milky sky.

5

Resthaven

The sows usually had two litters each year, in the spring and in the fall, and so twice a year, after weaning her piglets, every mother enjoyed what Mrs. Gobblespud had called a good rest. As soon as a newly weaned litter had "crossed the yard," the sow would expect the servant to open her door and then a gate at the upper end of the cluster of farm buildings. This gate was the entrance to a small field which the Pigman unimaginatively called the Pig Ground, but which the ladies always referred to as Resthaven.

"Not long now," a harassed mother would say to her neighbor at about the seventh week of nursing.

"Soon we'll be going to Resthaven. Not that I won't miss the kiddies."

"No, but you have to get away. Besides, it gives that lazy Pigman time to give the house a good cleaning."

Resthaven was a small triangular patch of rough hillside, sloping down from a point at the top to a long base bounded by a brook. The other two sides were fenced with pig wire, and right in the center stood a great old oak. Most of the upper part of the little field was dotted with ant heaps.

The morning after Daggie's brothers and sisters had left, the Pigman came to Number Five and opened the door. Normally on these occasions one or two heads might pop up along the row, and one or two shouts be heard of "Have a nice time!" But this time it was different, for no one remembered a piglet ever going to Resthaven, much less a dag. By the time Daggie had politely said good-bye to Auntie Swiller and Auntie Gobblespud, every other head was up to get a look at this strange baby. As Mrs. Barleylove made her stately way off after the lumbering servant, with Daggie trotting behind her, many and heartfelt were the good wishes that followed them, though softly spoken so as not to wake the Squire.

For Daggie, everything was new and wonderful. No sooner had the servant closed the gate than the little piglet cried, "Oh, Mommy! Isn't it exciting? Can I go off and explore?"

"Go where you like, darling," said his mother. "But be careful of the water at the bottom of the field. Pigs can't swim, you know."

Pigs might fly, though, thought Daggie Dogfoot gleefully to himself as he ran off over the summer grass. Especially if they could find somewhere high enough to jump off.

Mrs. Barleylove, watching her darling with pride, was quite amazed to see how fast he made his way around Resthaven. When Daggie arrived at the very top of the wedge-shaped field, he climbed up on the highest of all the ant heaps. He turned to face downhill and saw his mother looking up toward him. "Watch me, Mommy!" he yelled, and leaped off. He nose-dived into the grass, turned a somersault, rolled over a few times on the steep slope, and landed on the next ant heap six feet away.

"Yes, dear. Very clever," called Mrs. Barleylove tenderly, and went to the oak to look for acorns.

By the end of that first thrilling day, Daggie was pretty sore. He had climbed onto and jumped off everything he could find, every bank and ridge in the rough field, every ant heap, and several stumps of felled elms. But every effort had resulted in a crash landing, and now, in the warmth of the August evening, he was not only bruised but a little despondent.

He and his mother had just left a shallow place at the edge of the brook, where they had drunk their fill, and now they stood together at a point farther along the bank, a high point where the stream had cut away the side over the years as it made a swirling turn. Here they were about fifteen feet above the water, and behind them the slope of Resthaven was steep and short-grassed for some distance.

Suppose I started back up there and ran really fast, thought Daggie. "Mommy," he said, "did you say pigs couldn't swim?"

Mrs. Barleylove, like all her kind, had been brought up to believe the old sows' tale that a pig attempting to swim will cut its own throat by the awkward action of its sharp-hooved forefeet, and she explained this to her son. She was comfortably full of acorns and roots and grasses and berries, as well as the ration of pignuts the servant had brought, and she gazed dreamily down at the winking water without really thinking what she was saying.

"But I haven't got . . ." began Daggie, and then some instinct checked him.

"What, dear?" said Mrs. Barleylove absently.

"Er—I haven't heard that before," said Daggie quickly. "I mean, I didn't know that."

"There are lots of things you don't know, my son," said his mother in the way mothers always do.

And there's something that you don't know, too, thought the dag to himself. Which is that if I started back up there and ran really fast . . . Pigs *might* fly, he said to himself, Auntie Gobblespud said so. I just wish I had the chance to consult an expert before trying. Daggie had thought a good deal about getting expert advice and had often asked the birds who hopped around Number Five. But the sparrows, when he questioned them, only answered, "Cheep! Cheep!" in an impudent way, and the starlings simply piped rudely at him. Once a big crow had perched on the sty wall, but in reply to the piglet's questions only said, "Garn!"

Suddenly, as he stood by his mother high above the brook, there was a whistle of wings, and over their heads flew a black-and-white bird with a bright red bill and cheek patches and wide webbed feet with sharp claws at the ends of the toes. Beating its wings rapidly, it braked and dropped on the surface in a shower of water drops that gleamed golden in the sunlight. Wagging its tail feathers from side to side, it swam rapidly about. It drank and then showered itself with water by splashing with its wings.

Flying *and* swimming, thought Daggie. Too much!

"What's that bird, Mommy?" he asked. "I've never seen one like that before."

"There are lots of things you've never seen before, dear," said his mother in the way mothers always do. "That's a duck."

"Where does it come from?" asked Daggie.

"Oh, Pigman keeps some," said Mrs. Barleylove. "For their eggs, I think. After all," she went on reflectively, "even servants have to eat, I suppose. Let them eat eggs."

"May I talk to it, Mommy?" said Daggie Dogfoot eagerly. "It won't hurt me, will it?"

"It won't hurt you," said his mother. "But I don't suppose you'll get much out of it. They're stupid things. Probably won't understand a word you say."

But when Daggie ran down to the shallow place and called to the duck, it immediately turned and swam toward him with a pleasant expression on its neat face.

6

Felicity

"Good-mor-ning-duck," said Daggie Dogfoot very slowly and loudly—the proper way to address foreigners. "May-I-ask-you-some-thing-please?" The duck, which had been walking toward him up the sandy shallows with a quick rolling gait, hopped onto a low willow branch, gripped it comfortably with her clawed feet, settled her feathers, and considered the piglet with bright eyes.

"Absolutely anything you like," she answered in a quiet musical voice.

"Oh," said Daggie, surprised, "Mommy said you wouldn't . . ." He stopped, confused.

". . . wouldn't understand a word you said?"

chuckled the duck. "Well, your mother obviously doesn't know much about Muscovy ducks."

Daggie gulped. "Please," he said, "what is a . . . Muscovy duck?"

"Well," said the duck, "we're a tree-perching variety—that's what these are for." She raised one foot to show the curved claws. "Originally from South America."

Daggie's world had expanded enormously since leaving Number Five, but it was still very small. He imagined South America to be the next field beyond Resthaven.

"Anyway," said the duck, "what did you want to ask me?"

Daggie took a deep breath. He looked up at the steep bank to see if his mother was there, but she had moved away.

"Do you think," he said slowly and carefully, "that pigs might fly?" The duck opened her bill wide, and then hastily closed it again. Then she opened and closed it rapidly perhaps a dozen times, making a soft quot-quot-quotting noise.

"Well, do you?" asked Daggie.

"I think," said the duck, "that almost anything *might* happen. Though I have never actually heard of a flying pig. Who put the idea in your head?"

"My auntie," said Daggie. "Well, she was our next-door neighbor, really, but I called her Auntie.

She said it, you see, and I'm pretty sure they were all talking about me."

"So it's you that's going to . . . fly?" said the Muscovy.

"Hope so."

"Have you tried yet?"

"Oh, yes, quite a few times. But I can't seem to get airborne. That's why I'm so excited about this place." And Daggie proceeded to explain to his new friend his idea of the steep downhill take-off and the leap from the top of the high bank into glorious soaring flight. "D'you think I could do it?" asked Daggie Dogfoot.

The bright-eyed duck looked thoughtfully at this strange creature before her. She looked at his big head and his hard thin little body and his skinny backside. She looked down at the sand and saw the three sets of prints in it—her own webs, the deep slots of the heavy sow, and the third strange set of tracks of two tiny slots and two pawmarks. The idea of a modest lecture on the qualities necessary for flight occurred to her, but she dismissed it immediately in the face of the determination that shone on the piglet's features.

"I think you're going to try," she said. And looking at the deep pool the current had gouged out below the steep bank, she added, "It's not a bad place to try, either. I assume you can swim?"

Daggie looked puzzled.

"Pigs can't swim," he said. "I'd have thought you'd know that. I'm not talking about swimming. I'm talking about flying."

The duck hopped off the willow branch and walked over to Daggie. Pretending to dig in the damp sand with her bill, she shot a close look at the piglet's forefeet. I wonder, she thought. His high-flown ambitions are going to flop, that's for sure. But something else quite novel might come out of it.

"Tell you what," she said. "I'd love to see the—er—maiden flight. Would you mind?"

"Not a bit," Daggie replied excitedly. "That's exactly what I wanted—an expert to be around to give me tips. I mean it isn't just the take-off. I may need some help with landing."

Once again the duck made that soft quot-quot-quotting noise with her bill.

"Yes," she said. "Though coming down is really the easiest part. By the way, what does your mother think about all this?"

"Oh, she doesn't know," said Daggie. "I thought I'd try it very early in the morning while she's still asleep. How about tomorrow?"

"All right," said the duck. "I'll be in the pool here at sunrise tomorrow. By the way, I don't know your name."

"Daggie Dogfoot," said the piglet.

"Right," said the duck. She slipped into the water and began to paddle off upstream.

"Wait a minute," Daggie called after her. "How will you get here that early? Won't you have to wait till Pigman lets you out?"

The duck stopped paddling and floated back toward him on the current.

"Pigman?" she said.

"Yes, the servant," said Daggie. "You know, that dirty fat man."

"Oh, you mean Duckman," said the Muscovy. "Oh, no, I don't go in the shed at night with the rest of them. I roost in a tree."

You might suppose Duckman just keeps us for the eggs we lay, she thought, but I've seen him before now go into the shed with an empty sack and come out with it full and kicking. I'm not taking any risks. And off she swam again. She was almost around the next bend in the stream before Daggie realized he did not know her name. He ran through the shallow water onto the bank and galloped along till he caught up with her.

"What's your name?" he shouted down.

"Felicity," said the duck.

"That's a funny name," shouted Daggie. "What's it mean?"

"Happiness," said the duck, and paddled away past the boundary of Resthaven and out of the piglet's sight.

Happiness, thought Daggie as he made his way toward his mother, who was lying under the oak tree. Life seems to be full of it. Living in this lovely place, and making such a nice friend, and tomorrow . . . wheeeee!

Mrs. Barleylove woke up from her nap at his squealing arrival. "Where have you been, baby?" she asked. "Talking to that duck?" She grunted with amusement.

"Yes, Mommy," said Daggie excitedly, "and she's awfully nice, and she's called Felicity, and"—he took a deep breath—"she's a Muscovy from South America."

"That's nice," said Mrs. Barleylove. "You come and take a rest now. You don't want to overtire yourself. Tomorrow's another day."

But as Daggie Dogfoot lay by his mother's side

and dozed in the sheltered warmth of Resthaven while the afternoon shadows lengthened, he knew that tomorrow wasn't just another day. Tomorrow was the day he had been planning for ages and ages, a whole two weeks, a quarter of his life. Tomorrow was the day he would fly. And Felicity would be there to help him. His mouth spread in a grin of pure joy, he fell soundly asleep.

7

Gosh!

Felicity woke early the next morning on her usual perch. This was the thin branch of an alder tree sticking out over the stream. She had chosen it not only because it was completely fox-proof, but because she liked the never-ending music of the running water, singing her to sleep with its bubbling lullaby and waking her each day with its gurgling song.

She stretched her wings, one after the other, pushing out each in its turn to its fullest extent so that the big flight feathers stood apart from one another, as a human might stretch his fingers wide. Then she flapped her wings vigorously as she stood on the branch and shook herself all over. She felt very happy.

She began to think about her new friend, Daggie Dogfoot. He's going to get a ducking, she thought with amusement, and then it suddenly struck her that a ducking might easily turn into a drowning. She jumped off her alder branch and flew rapidly downstream toward Resthaven. She was suddenly worried that the piglet might have been too impatient to wait for her.

However, as soon as she reached the little sloping field, she could see that everything was in order. Under the oak lay a mountain of spotted flesh, which was Mrs. Barleylove still asleep. And at the top of the steep slope above the high bank, a small spotty figure danced with impatience, pawing at the ground with his round front feet as though he were a puppy on an invisible leash.

"Hello, Felicity!" cried Daggie as the duck glided over his head. "Take-off in two minutes. O.K.?"

A minute and three-quarters later the first rays of the rising sun came over the eastern bank of Resthaven and shone on the rough bark of the oak tree and on the smooth, closed, white-lashed eyelids of Mrs. Barleylove. She opened her eyes, stretched, heaved herself to her feet, and looked around for her beloved boy. She had hardly focused on him, high above her on the slope, when, to her absolute horror, she saw him begin to run downhill at great speed, faster, faster, faster, till at last he leaped out over the high bank of the stream and disappeared from her sight.

Felicity had positioned herself close under the Resthaven bank of the brook, directly underneath the take-off point. She knew that the impetus of his downhill run would take Daggie well out into the middle of the pool, and, head cocked upward, she waited, ready to go instantly to his aid.

Suddenly the quiet of the morning was shattered by an anguished scream from the horrified watcher under the oak tree, and in the same instant, high above the waiting duck, a small spotted shape shot out from the top of the bank and seemed for a frozen fraction of time to hang suspended against the clear blue sky. Legs working frantically, ears streaming behind his head, ridiculous tail whipping around and around like an eggbeater, Daggie Dogfoot enjoyed a split second of level flight. Then his heavy head came down to point him at the pool, a squeal of fright burst from him as the dark water rushed up to greet him, and, "Eeeeeeeek—kersplosh—glug!"—he was gone from view.

When he rose to the surface, he was facing the opposite bank and could not see the reassuring figure of the Muscovy duck, who by now had swum close to him. He could see nothing but what seemed an ocean of water, of which he had already swallowed a lot, and on top of the newfound knowledge that pigs couldn't fly came the awful realization that they couldn't swim either. He knew this. Mommy had said so. Mommy, whom he would never see again.

"Heeeelp!" he squealed. "Heee-gurgle-glug!" and down he went again.

As soon as he surfaced for the second time he

heard two voices. One was his mother's, shouting desperately from the shallows where she stood belly-deep after a thundering gallop from the oak tree.

"Save him! Save my boy!" yelled Mrs. Barleylove in agony.

The other was a quiet voice which spoke in his ear.

"Keep still," said the quiet voice. "Don't struggle. Don't talk. Keep your mouth tight shut. Breathe through your snout. Run after me. Just run as though you were on dry land," and Felicity set off for the far bank, which was by now the nearer of the two. She wagged her tail encouragingly and glanced back over her shoulder at the piglet.

Because of the confidence in the duck's voice, because even in the midst of his panic he still had spirit and courage, and because there was nothing else to do, Daggie obeyed. He clenched his teeth, tipped up his head so that his nostrils pointed skyward like the twin guns of a surfaced submarine, kicked with his hind legs and paddled like mad with his doggy feet, trying hard to imagine that he was galloping through the grass.

To his amazement, he began to move forward through the water after the duck, at first slowly, then faster as he gained momentum and confidence, and finally so fast that, before they reached the far bank, he was even with her and they touched bottom together in a little reedy inlet.

They looked at each other and their eyes shone, Felicity's with amusement and pleasure, Daggie's with relief and triumph as realization swept over him.

"Pigs can't fly," said Daggie. Felicity shook her head.

"But there's one pig," said Daggie quietly, "that can," said Daggie more loudly, "swim!" shouted Daggie Dogfoot at the top of his squeaky voice, and off he went, all by himself, toward his mother on the Resthaven bank.

Mrs. Barleylove had continued throughout to yell, "Save my boy!" pausing only when it seemed he had reached safety. Now here he was back in deep water again, and she began to squeal as before, until two voices reached her ears.

"Calm yourself, madam," said one voice, as the duck, who had flown quickly across over the head of the swimmer, landed beside her. "He's all right. Just listen to him." And as the sow quieted, she heard the other voice, the voice of her fast-approaching son.

"Mommy! Mommy!" came the cry over the gentle lapping of the pool. "Look at me! I can swim! It's easy! Watch!" and as she stared, open-mouthed, the small figure came paddling nearer and nearer, pushing up a little bow wave in front of it with the speed of its progress.

Still Mrs. Barleylove did not really understand what had happened since the sun had awakened her. As soon as Daggie was out of the brook and shaking himself like a water spaniel, she turned and made off up the bank toward the summit, scolding as she went in the way that mothers do when their children have given them a bad fright.

"Silly boy!" she said. "Naughty boy! Come quickly and run around in the sunshine or you'll catch your death of cold. I told you not to go down by the water. You're never to go there again, understand? Never. I don't know what your father would say if he knew," and so on, until, receiving no reply, she turned and found that she had been talking to herself.

Slowly the incredible truth dawned on Mrs. Barleylove. Her poor undersized deformed child was

swimming, really swimming, swimming beautifully. "Special feet for some purpose," eh? If only the
neighbors could see him now!

"Oh, Daggie darling!" she called down. "How
clever you are!"

How happy I am, thought Daggie, to have such a
lovely mother, to swim in this beautiful sparkling
stuff, to be with my friend whose very name means
happiness. And he paddled around wildly, while
every little fish in the pool formed its mouth into a
perfect round "O" of wonder. The rails in the reeds
tut-tutted their amazement. The heron at the top of
a downstream willow squawked his disbelief. A
brilliant kingfisher gave an admiring whistle, and a
passing green woodpecker laughed hysterically. And
up the line of the brook flew a solitary swan, the
sound of his great wings expressing exactly the
surprise of all. "Gosh!" was the noise they made.
"Gosh! Gosh! Gosh! Gosh!"

8
The Truth Comes Out

The news traveled fast, by air mail of course, for the woodpecker shouted it to his mate in her nesting hole, and starlings resting in upper branches heard it. Later they discussed it in wheezy whistles as they bathed in the yard trough. Sparrows, searching the floor for small seeds, listened to the starlings, and then, of course, told everybody. By midday there was only one creature who did not know the story of the swimming piglet, and that, of course, was the Pigman, too stupid to understand animal language. The Squire knew, as the sows soon found out.

Mrs. Swiller and Mrs. Gobblespud were conversing across the empty outer run of Number Five, now brushed and scraped and washed clean by the servant, and smelling strongly of disinfectant. They were recalling a conversation of a few weeks ago.

"Do you recall what she said, Mrs. G.?" grunted Mrs. Swiller.

"That I do, Mrs. S.," replied Mrs. Gobblespud, "that I do. Special, she said. Special feet, that's what she said. And do you remember what we said?"

"That I do, Mrs. G.," answered Mrs. Swiller. "Sure as my name's Rosie Swiller, I do. 'Special feet for some purpose,' that's what we asked if she meant. Nonsense, we thought."

"Just imagine!" said Mrs. Gobblespud. She paused. "Always said he was a clever little chap," she went on.

"Brave, too," said Mrs. Swiller.

"Never heard of any Ploughbarrow pig swimming, never."

"Never heard of any pig swimming."

"What'll Pigman say when he finds out?"

There was a short silence, and then with one horrified voice they said, "What'll Squire say when he finds out?"

The words were hardly out of their mouths when they heard the deep grunt and the rattle of the door on the other side of the yard. Mrs. Swiller and Mrs. Gobblespud slid back off their walls and stood very still in their sties, heads lowered, breath held. If they had had fingers, they would have crossed them. Neither wanted in the least to hear her name called if the boar started asking questions. As it turned out, no one was to escape.

"Ladies!" barked the Squire in his loudest voice. "A word with you all, if you please. My apologies if any of you are in the midst of your duties, but I want you all on parade in one minute."

At these stern words there was a tremendous noise of hustling and bustling and shuffling mixed with the squeals of rudely disturbed piglets, and within thirty seconds eight pairs of trotters reared up onto eight front doors, and above them eight large, anxious faces peered across at the lord and master.

Only at Number Five, of course, was there no face, and it seemed to the nervous sows that the Squire's angry gaze was directed at this space rather than at any one of them. After a moment, however, he shifted his look to Number One, and then slowly, deliberately, swung his heavy head to scrutinize in turn each face, all the way to Number Nine.

At last he spoke. "It has come to my attention," he said, "that something very strange has been going on, doncherknow. What?"

No one answered, so he went on. "Now I'm going to get to the bottom of this, so I shall ask each of you in turn. And I don't want any shilly-shallying. Understand?"

"Yes, Squire," chorused eight worried voices.

The Squire looked directly at Number One again. "Mrs. Troughlicker," he said, "the sparrows are talking about a swimming pig. What do you know about it?"

"Not a great deal, Squire," said Mrs. Troughlicker uncomfortably. "There are rumors."

"Mrs. Swiller?"

Mrs. Swiller hesitated, and glanced nervously across at Mrs. Gobblespud.

"Well, Mrs. Swiller?"

"It isn't one of mine, Squire. They're all here, dry as a bone, every one," and Mrs. Swiller forced a kind of snorting laugh.

"No laughing matter," said the Squire severely. "Mrs. Gobblespud?"

"Pigs can't swim, Squire, we all know that," said Mrs. Gobblespud in a strained voice. "Not if they're normal," she added thoughtlessly.

"Normal? Normal?" said the Squire loudly. "What child of mine has ever been other than normal? What are you talking about? What's she talking about, Mrs. Maizemunch?"

"Don't know, Squire."

"Mrs. Grubguzzle?"

"Don't ask me, Squire."

"But I do ask you," shouted the Squire angrily. "I do ask you! I'm asking all of you. Except, of course,

Mrs. Barleylove," and he shifted his gaze back to the door of Number Five.

Nobody said anything.

"Well, she's at Resthaven, isn't she?" asked the Squire. Eight heads nodded. The Squire began to lose patience again.

"You're not telling me," he shouted, "that Mrs. Barleylove's been swimming in the brook, are you?"

Eight heads shook and eight faces struggled to
keep straight at this question.

"Well then!" roared the Squire. "I saw her last
litter cross the yard with my own eyes, and a fine
bunch they were. Any father would be proud of
them. And," he added as an afterthought, "any
mother, too. So if she's not swimming, and she has
no youngsters with her, will you kindly tell me who
in the name of Saint Anthony is this swimming
pig?"

Now Saint Anthony is the patron saint of pigmen,
and when the sows heard the Squire swear so
dreadfully, they knew that the issue could no longer
be avoided. It would have to come out sometime. It
had better come out now.

"Well?" said the Squire.

"Well, Squire," said Mrs. Swiller and Mrs. Gobblespud together. "This last litter, Mrs. Barleylove
. . . had a . . . dag," they finished in a kind of
whisper.

There was an awful silence, broken only by the
sound of the Squire grinding his tusks. The sows
could not see his eyes, hidden by his drooping ears,
and of this they were glad.

At last he spoke, very softly. "Go on," he said.

Mrs. Swiller swallowed. "Usually, you see,
Squire," she said, "when a . . . dag's born . . ."

"Usually?" interrupted the Squire in the same soft voice.

"Doesn't happen very often, of course," put in Mrs. Gobblespud hastily, "but most of us, one time or another . . ."

"I see," said the Squire heavily.

"And then," said Mrs. Swiller, "the servant takes it away."

"Takes it away?"

"Well, the mother never does see it any more."

"But this one came back!" said Mrs. Gobblespud excitedly, and at this the rest could not contain themselves but joined in in a babble of voices.

"Wouldn't be beat!"

"Squeezed under the door!"

"Then Pigman came again!"

"Dirty fat man!"

"We told him!"

"And later on he came again!"

"When the others crossed the yard!"

"And she told him!"

At last the hubbub died down, and there was silence again, this time unbroken.

After a while the Squire spoke. It seemed to the sows that he sounded old and tired.

"This . . . dag, then," he said slowly, "is down at Resthaven with Mrs. Barleylove?"

"Yes, Squire," they all replied.

"It must be the swimmer, then?"

"Yes, Squire."

"Extraordinary. Extraordinary. Boy or girl?"

"Boy, Squire."

"Boy, eh? What's he called?"

"Daggie Dogfoot."

"Daggie what?"

"Dogfoot."

"Because . . . ?"

"Yes, Squire."

"Which is presumably how he . . . ?"

Eight heads nodded, and nine minds imagined the scene in the brook. "Extraordinary," said the Squire.

His natural courtesy reasserted itself, and he said in his normal bluff, hearty voice, "I'm obliged to you, ladies. Please return to your duties, doncherknow."

But after the sows had disappeared from sight, the boar still leaned on his gate. He felt shocked. But he also felt in some way relieved, for it is better to admit some facts, even hard, bitter facts, than to go on pretending that they don't exist. Most of all perhaps, as he stood there in the late afternoon sunshine, he began to feel proud.

Daggie Dogfoot, eh? he thought to himself. Taken

away but fought his way back. And swimming! Swimming like a fish, apparently! Extraordinary! By Saint Anthony, said the Squire to himself, I'd like to meet the little guy.

9

The Race

Daggie spent nearly all that day in the water, coming out only for a drink of milk or to eat some of the pignuts the servant threw down. The Pigman noticed nothing. We see only what we expect to see, and he did not dream that he was a slave of a swimming pig.

Mrs. Barleylove had already come to look on Felicity as a combination nurse, aunt, instructress, and lifeguard. Mrs. Barleylove stood on the bank watching teacher and pupil with a silly grin on her big fat face.

Felicity concentrated on Daggie's streamlining, to begin with. She wanted him lower in the water, but he was having trouble with his nose. Like all pigs, his nostrils faced directly forward out of the flat end of his snout and the water simply rushed up into them.

"Why doesn't the water go up *your* nose?" spluttered Daggie, after much trial and error.

"Oh, we've got a sort of valve thing we can shut to stop it," said the duck. "Just as you can shut your eyes if you don't want to see something." She paused, considering. "Perhaps you've got one too?" she said.

"Try and see," called Mrs. Barleylove. "After all, my dear," she addressed Felicity, "I can put my snout deep in a trough full of slops and gobble away without having to take it out."

So Daggie tried, first on dry land, thinking very hard about pinching the insides of his nostrils together, while Felicity peered up his nose. After a while she thought it was working, so they went in the water, and it was!

Then Felicity redesigned Daggie's swimming action. His otter-like forefeet were just fine for the job. But his hind feet, used as though running on dry land, lacked the necessary drive.

The duck taught him to stick his hind legs straight out behind him and beat them up and down in the water alternately, as fast as he could, keeping them stiff, barely breaking the surface.

They reached this stage by the end of the first day, and a long day it seemed to a very tired piglet curling up by his mother's warm side under the oak tree at dusk.

Oddly enough, as the Muscovy was settling to sleep on her alder branch, she heard, farther up the valley, a thin, hard cry in the coming darkness. "I-zaak!" it sounded like. "I-zaak!" Must warn Daggie about otters, she thought drowsily. Don't want him mistaken for a big fish.

For the next few days they worked hard at improving Daggie's style, and on the morning of the fourth day Felicity swam down early from her alder tree and found Daggie already practicing in the pool.

"Hello, Felicity!" shouted Daggie. "I've just been warming up. You said something about a final trial today."

"Well," said Felicity, "I thought we might have a race. I mean you've taken to the water like a duck, as the saying goes. Let's see if you can beat one."

"Hey!" Daggie said. "You're a real swimmer. You've been doing it all your life. I'm only a beginner. You'll wallop me."

I'm not so sure of that, thought the Muscovy.

"It's just for fun," she said. "Just to see how you perform over a longer distance. I thought we could start from the end of the pool and swim upstream as far as the Resthaven boundary fence. The current's not running all that strongly because we haven't had rain for a long time. And it's a pretty straight course. About two hundred yards overall, I think. O.K.?"

"I'm game," said Daggie. "Wait while I get Mommy to watch."

"Well, don't bring her here," said Felicity. "Ask her if she'd be kind enough to go to the finish line. Ask her to stand on the bank by the fence and act as judge."

Five minutes later duck and pig floated side by side at the lower end of the pool. They saw the big spotted shape of Mrs. Barleylove come down to the bank and stand waiting. A little way up the kingfisher sat on his root.

"We'll use him as a starting signal," said Felicity. "When he moves, swim."

They fixed their eyes on the blazing little bird, and Daggie braced his hind feet against the bank behind him, ready to push off to a good start. He quivered all over with excitement.

Suddenly, in a burning streak of color, the kingfisher flashed away upstream, and they were off!

For a time they were even, and Felicity, thrusting as hard as she could with her broad webbed feet, began to think that she had overestimated this prodigy, for though she could see out of the corner of her eye that he was swimming beautifully, doing in perfect style everything that he'd been taught, she felt she had the better of him. For a moment she even considered slacking off a bit, to let him win and give him confidence. Then she caught his eye, and it seemed to have a twinkle in it.

Suddenly, at about the halfway stage, Daggie

Dogfoot changed gears, and Felicity realized that he'd only been playing with her. Twice as low as before his body went in the water, twice as hard as before those otter's feet pulled, twice as fast as before those outstretched hind legs beat, and he shot away in front of her with the speed of a salmon. She could hear Mrs. Barleylove behaving as an impartial judge certainly should not, urging Daggie on to further efforts with loud proud squeals, and she saw her jump for joy, all four feet off the ground, as he crossed the finish line, fifty yards ahead.

By the time the duck finished, the piglet had been able to climb out of the brook, shake himself all over, be licked by the judge, and call encouragement to his puffing, panting teacher. He isn't even out of breath, thought Felicity as she clambered out and waddled up to mother and son.

"How about that, madam?" she puffed. "Aren't you proud of him?"

"Any mother would be," said Mrs. Barleylove. And any father, too, she thought. At least I hope he will.

10

Izaak

A mile upstream was a mill, the very mill that ground the barley meal for the pigs, and beside it was a great pond that gave the waterpower to drive the mill wheel. It was from this pond, some nights before, that the thin, hard cry had reached Felicity's ears as she dropped off to sleep. The animal that had made the cry was a big otter, in the best of health and the worst of tempers. And the reason for his anger had been his lack of success in realizing a long-held ambition.

The millpond was deep and dark, with a bed made of thick mud and the rotting of a million leaves dropped into it over many autumns. Big fish lived in it, tench and carp and pike; and of these last there was one absolute monster, so otter lore had it, a pike half as long as a man, as fierce as a wolf and twice as cunning. Often in his travels between the sea and the hills, this particular otter had spent some time by the millpond with one idea in mind—to find this monster and kill him and eat him. And on that particular night he had come close to doing it.

Searching the deepest, darkest corner of the thickest tangle of weeds, the otter had suddenly seen, motionless beneath him, a long barred shape with narrow wolf jaws and cold, hard eyes, a shape even longer than himself—and he was thirty inches from the end of his nose to the tip of his rudder.

Quick as he was, the long barred shape was quicker, leaving behind it a swirling fog of rotten leaves and a cloud of soupy water and strings of gas bubbles and an angry otter.

"I-zaak!" the otter had cried in his fury as he hauled himself out by the black oak sluice gates all slimy with mosses. "I-zaak!"

The otter spent several days by the millpond, enjoying some easy fishing but without further sight of the monster pike. And then, on the day after Daggie and Felicity had had their race, he decided to move on downstream.

He slipped down with the last of the night, past the farm buildings, under Felicity asleep on her alder branch, past the finishing line of the race, and into the reach that led to the pool beneath the high bank. Sometimes he swam on the surface; sometimes only a string of bubbles showed his progress.

But suddenly he saw something that not only made him lift his round tomcat's head right up out of the water, but actually land and stand up in the grass on his hind legs, peering and sniffing and moving his head from side to side as though he simply could not believe his eyes. In the pool ahead, swimming rapidly from side to side with a racing turn at either bank, was a pig! It wasn't a very big pig by the look of it, no longer than the otter's body without its rudder, but it was, undoubtedly, a white pig with black spots. And it was, undoubtedly, swimming.

Now otters have a tremendous, if rather twisted, sense of humor, and they love jokes, especially bad jokes. One of the jokes that this otter enjoyed very much was giving people sudden awful frights. As everyone knows, a good way to give someone a sudden awful fright is to appear, from nowhere, when you're least expected, and, better still, to make a fearful noise at the same time. A big grin came over the otter's face, and he dropped down and slid into and under the water.

Daggie was in the exact middle of the pool, swimming along without a care in the world in the peaceful silence of the early morning, when sudden-ly, right beside him, a grinning whiskery face popped up, opened a wide mouth to show a battery of sharp white teeth, and shouted, right in his ear, "I-ZAAK!"

Daggie felt three sorts of feelings, all at the same time. Startled because of the sudden noise, afraid because of the rows of teeth, and angry because he was startled and afraid. Of the three he quickly decided that he was mostly angry, and he trod water and said in a shrill, breathless voice, "I don't know who you are, but this is my pool and you have no manners frightening people like that, and I'll tell my Mommy and Felicity, and anyway your breath stinks of fish."

Now otters make all sorts of noises, from loud ones when they are angry or want to frighten some-one, through chitterings and chatterings, to lovely fluty whistles when they are playing or calling to one another from afar. But when they think something is really very funny, they laugh quite silently.

To Daggie's astonishment, that is what the crea-ture in front of him proceeded to do, splitting his hairy face wide open, and rocking to and fro in the water with his webbed forepaws clasped against his chest. He laughed so much and rocked about so wildly that eventually he sank below the water and swallowed some mouthfuls. Spitting and puffing, he came back to the surface and at last calmed himself enough to speak to the piglet.

"Sorry, old pig," he spluttered, still grinning broadly. "Sorry if I scared you."

By now Daggie had gotten his breath back, and he said with a sort of quiet dignity, "I'm not an old pig, I'm a young pig. And I'm not just a pig, I'm a pedigree Gloucester Old Spots. And my name is Daggie Dogfoot, son of Champion Imperial Challenger III of Ploughbarrow."

The otter's mouth fell wider and wider open during this recital, but whether in astonishment or in preparation for another round of silent laughter Daggie never knew, for at that instant there was a whistle of wings and Felicity splashed down between them.

She had been so busy with Daggie's training that she had quite forgotten to mention the subject of otters to him, as she had realized with horror when this one's shout had awakened her. Now she faced the danger bravely, determined to protect her little friend. There was a moment's pause, and then all three animals spoke at the same time.

"Are you all right, Daggie?" said Felicity. "Who in the water is he?" said Daggie. And "Hello, old duck," said the otter, and dived beneath the surface.

As the friends swam rather rapidly to the Resthaven bank, they answered each other's questions.

"Yes, I'm all right," said Daggie. "Why shouldn't I be?"

"Because that's an otter," said Felicity. "Great hunter. Kills anything and everything that swims —fish, frogs, eels, ducklings. Never heard of it bothering piglets, but then piglets don't usually swim. You'd better keep away from him."

"Well, he didn't hurt me," said Daggie. "He just seemed to find me rather funny. I can't think why."

As they talked, they could see strings of bubbles bobbing up as the otter searched the pool, and after a moment more he surfaced, smooth as oil, and walked out onto the sandy hollow below them.

"No fish in there, old pig," said the otter cheerfully, "and don't say there are, 'cause there aren't. Must have driven them away with all that swimming practice of yours. What's a pig doing swimming anyway, old duck?"

"I taught him," said Felicity shortly. "What's your name, if I might ask?"

"Izaak," said the otter. "And don't think it isn't, 'cause it is. My friends call me Ike, and don't say they don't, 'cause they do."

There was something very nice about the otter, despite his fearful fishy breath. Perhaps it was his cheeriness. Perhaps it was his odd way of speaking. Or maybe it was the growing certainty that he was not in fact an enemy to them that made the two friends suddenly warm to him.

"Sorry I spoke so rudely to you, Mr. Izaak," said Daggie, "but you did give me an awful shock."

"That's all right, old pig," said the otter. "I'm fond of a good laugh and don't say I'm not, 'cause I am." He turned to Felicity. "Going back to this business of him"—he nodded at Daggie—"swimming. From what I could see, he's pretty good on the surface. I never expected to see a pig swim, old duck, let alone swim as well as that, and don't say I did, 'cause I didn't."

"Yes, he is good," said Felicity. "But then he's lucky enough to have been born specially equipped," and she pointed with her bill to Daggie's forefeet.

"Let's have a look, old pig," said the otter, and

after a close examination he sat back with a long, low whistle, and looked thoughtfully at the piglet.

"Tell you what," he said. "I was going to the seashore for a break, but I'm not in a hurry. Now am I right in thinking you haven't done much underwater work?"

"Not much," said Daggie. "Just the surface dive."

"It's nearly all been surface work," said Felicity. "I'm afraid I'm not much good down below."

"No, but I am," said the otter.

"And don't say you aren't . . ." said Daggie quickly.

". . . because you are," finished Felicity, and they all laughed in their different ways, the otter silently, the duck quot-quotting, the piglet giving little squeals.

"Seriously," said the otter, "I could teach you a lot, old pig, if you'd like. You have no webs, and no rudder to speak of, so you'll be a bit slow on the turn. But I could teach you a lot about breath control and use of currents and general aquabatics. We'd have you catching big fish in no time."

"Well," said Daggie doubtfully, "I'd love to have lessons from you, Mr. Izaak, but I don't actually eat fish."

"Nonsense!" said Felicity sharply. "You mean you haven't eaten fish—yet. Just think, if this gentleman is kind enough to teach you . . . after all, pigs are omnivorous."

"What's that mean, old duck?" said the otter.

"Means they can eat anything and everything."

"She's clever, isn't she, old pig?" said the otter. "They say eating fish is good for your brains, though it doesn't seem to have done me much good," and he swished around in another fit of silent laughter.

So it came about that Daggie Dogfoot acquired a second teacher and right away began more lessons, so that by the time Mrs. Barleylove, who had slept through everything, rolled down to the brook for her morning drink, she found Daggie was more under the water than on it. And often when his head popped up, there was a round brown whiskery one beside it, and sometimes his squeaks of delight mingled with the stranger's lovely fluty whistles. Felicity explained everything to her, and because it was all right with Felicity, it was all right with her.

All that day Daggie played with and learned from his new tutor, occasionally coming to the bank to see if his old tutor approved and was not upset, and she did and she wasn't, and his mother beamed her usual fatuous smile of pride.

In the afternoon swimmers and spectators moved upstream a little, and the otter caught a big trout, taking it in a lightning upward swirl too fast for the eye to follow. He pulled it onto the bank and offered Daggie first bite ("From the shoulder—the flesh is sweetest there, old pig"). Daggie was too polite to refuse and afterward glad that he hadn't, for it was delicious. Between them they ate most of the best of it, as they were hungry from their exertions. When they had returned to the brook, Mrs. Barleylove ate the rest—head, tail, bones, and all—till not a scale was left.

When the light began to fade, the otter said he must be going.

"See you tomorrow, old pig," he said. "You're learning fast."

"Oh, I really enjoyed that," said Daggie. "The underwater training, and the trout, and, of course, meeting you. Thank you so much, Mr. Izaak."

"Good night, old pig," said the otter. "But I told you before, and don't say that I didn't, 'cause I did—my friends call me Ike."

"Thanks, Ike," said Daggie happily.

11

The Flood

Daggie did not see his new friend Ike the next day, because overnight the weather, which controls everything in the country, changed completely. As Felicity had said before the race, they hadn't had rain for a long time. But not an hour after the otter had slipped away upstream, the heavens opened and proceeded to make up for their stinginess by such a display of generosity as none of the animals had ever known before. It rained heavily all that night, and went on without stopping for two more days and nights.

The sows in their sties kept to their inner compartments, venturing into their soaking outer runs only for food. The Squire, of course, was dry under his veranda roof, but the constant stream of water flowing across the yard from higher ground worried him. He was not concerned for himself, but he couldn't help thinking about the strange son of whose existence he had just heard. He hoped that that existence would not be ended in an untimely way, for he knew that boys will be boys, and this one sounded particularly adventurous. The brook will be swollen, thought the Squire. I hope the kid stays on dry land.

He spoke to the servant about it, but the Pigman, more hideous than ever in yellow oilskins and rain hat, was too stupid to understand his master.

At Number One and Number Two Mrs. Troughlicker and Mrs. Boltapple stood upright at their front doors and looked anxiously over the yard. It was covered with a stream of fast-running water, as indeed were the outer runs of all the sties. Only inside, where each sow had a raised wooden platform six inches high, was there still a dry space for them and their piglets. Mrs. Troughlicker spoke first.

"I don't like it, Mrs. B.," she said in a worried voice. "I've never seen rain like this."

"What can we do?" asked Mrs. Troughlicker.

"I'll be butchered if I know," said Mrs. Boltapple. "If only the rain would stop!"

But the rain did not stop. On the contrary, even as

they spoke, it began to come down heavily again, and the ladies hastily retreated indoors.

The Pigman stood at the door of his shed and looked down at the water, now almost over the lower of the two concrete steps. Behind him he heard rats squeaking among the bins, and his red face grew redder at the sound of his enemies' voices. But even as he turned to reach up for his hardwood club and do battle, a big buck rat came running out of the gloom of the shed and scampered right over his boots and out the door. It fell into the water and swam rapidly away. And as the Pigman watched, open-mouthed, half a dozen more rats of all sizes dashed past him and into the water and away. Something he had heard long ago, at school perhaps, came into his mind. A sinking ship, he thought. Rats leaving a sinking ship.

At that instant the westerly wind, which had been blowing hard from the sea far down at the foot of the valley, dropped for a moment, and in the ensuing lull the Pigman heard a sound from the other direction, from the upper eastern end. It was a muttering that grew to a grumbling that grew to a mighty rumbling. Straining his eyes through the driving rain, he stared back at the brook to where it curved into view around some trees two fields away.

Suddenly, to his horror, he saw a great wall of

brown water coming around this bend, and he knew in a flash what must have happened. The sluice gates have gone, thought the Pigman, the millpond's burst. And for once in his slow, lumbering life he acted quickly.

He grabbed a sack of pignuts, jumped off the steps of the shed into the six-inch-deep water, and splashed his way to the sties. He flung open door after door: Mrs. Troughlicker's, Mrs. Boltapple's, Mrs. Swedechopper's, Mrs. Swiller's, missing the empty Number Five, then Mrs. Gobblespud's, Mrs. Maizemunch's, Mrs. Grazegrass's, Mrs. Grubguzzle's. As the sows and litters ran out into the yard, he blundered across it to the store pens and fattening pens, throwing wide door after door till a hundred and fifty spotted shapes of all sizes were stampeding in the rushing flood. Only when he had opened the last door of all, the Squire's, did he allow himself one fearful glance over his shoulder. The wall of water was halfway across the last field in front of the buildings, and coming at the speed of a galloping horse.

The Pigman, like all his kind, knew that pigs are the most awkward animals in the world to drive, so he did the only thing he could. Handicapped though he was by his bulk and his boots and his long yellow oilskins and the sack of pignuts, he ran as hard as he could toward the gate that led to Resthaven, shouting at the top of his voice the pigkeeper's universal feeding call.

"PIG-pig-pig-pig-PIG-pig-pig-pig-PIG!" he yelled amid the noise of the rain and the renewed wind and the thundering of the watery threat behind them, and he pounded desperately toward the high ground at the top of the little triangular field.

And behind him rose two waves. One was white, spotted with black, and one was brown. One squealed with fear, and one roared with menace. One was moving as fast as it possibly could, but a pig cannot gallop half as speedily as a horse, and the other wave gained and gained on the first. As the last and slowest piglet struck the rising ground, the first and fastest wave of the flood was less than a sow's length from his curly little tail.

Then the flood turned before the hill and swept across the lower slopes of the field, smashing down the old oak tree from the place where it had stood for three hundred years and carrying it away like a matchstick. Twenty feet above Daggie's take-off place on the high bank went the oak, twisting and turning and thrashing its old arms in agony on its road to the windswept sea.

But the pigs were safe, not just all one hundred and fifty-one of them, but all one hundred and fifty-three. For the first thing the Pigman saw, when his pounding heart and bursting lungs had quieted a little, was a group of three figures standing at the very topmost point of Resthaven and staring at the great army of pigs covering the high slope. Old sow from Number Five's all right then, he thought. And that horrible little dag. Though Heaven knows what one of my ducks is doing with them.

There was noise all around them as they stood and panted on their hilltop refuge. The blustering shout of the wind competed with the menacing roar of the brook that had become a great river. On the waters of that river hissed the lash of the never-ending rain. At one moment Daggie imagined he heard, far out on the flood, an excited fluty whistle, as though someone were actually enjoying the storm. But suddenly, clear above the other noises, was heard a sharp cracking sound, and from the hill a hundred and fifty-five heads turned and three hundred and ten eyes looked back toward the homes they had left behind, to see the beginning of the first voyage of a strange craft.

The rats had been right to go, for the cracking noise proclaimed the launching of the Pigman's shed, as the flood lifted it bodily from its foundation. Past the drowned sties it came, over the submerged field gate, and out into the center of the great expanse of dark, sliding, eddying water that now stretched before the watchers. Its door hung open, as the pigman had left it when he ran to rescue them, and as the shed spun slowly in the current they

could see within it the great bins of barley meal and
middlings and flaked corn and the piled sacks of
pignuts, all sailing swiftly away to be food for the
fish in the sea.

Another story came into the Pigman's slow mind
from distant days in the village schoolroom. Looks
like the Ark, he thought. Trouble is, we aren't on it.
And all the food I have for them is this fifty-pound
sack of nuts. Still, they won't be short of water to
drink.

He went to the topmost point of Resthaven, and,
opening the sack, threw the pignuts far and wide
over the small triangle of field that was left high and

dry. Within half a minute everything was eaten, and the multitude was squealing for more, while far in the distance the shed sailed on downriver.

The Pigman folded the empty sack, placed it on top of an ant heap, and sat carefully down on it. He sat motionless, his head in his hands, while the pigs jostled and grumbled below him. If there had been anyone on any of the other hilltops nearby, it would have seemed a strange sight: above, the bright yellow spot of the man's oilskins and rain hat; below that, the spotted throng; and below them, the chocolate-colored flood, darkening from milk to plain as the daylight faded. Mrs. Barleylove and Daggie and Felicity still stood together.

"Poor old Duckman," said Felicity. "He looks all in."

"Duckman?" said Daggie absently. "Oh, you mean Pigman. Yes, he does. Still, he's a good and faithful servant, you know. He did his duty." Felicity had also been thinking of the story of the Flood, as the Ark-like shed had drifted by, but, being better educated than the man, remembered more of it. She began to make the quot-quot-quotting noise, which Daggie now knew well was her way of giggling.

"What's the joke?" said Daggie.

"I was thinking of a story," said Felicity. "In a book. Called the Bible. About a man called Noah."

"Why?" said Daggie. "Is Pigman like Noah?"

"No," said Felicity. "More like one of his sons."

"What was he called?" asked Daggie.

"Ham," said Felicity happily.

12

Going for Help

In the early light of the following morning the scene was quite different. To begin with, the flood was not quite as high, for the burst pond was empty now and it had not rained in the night. The water had receded far enough to show the gaping hole where the old oak used to stand, but it was still running very wide and very strong, and there was no sign of the outline of the brook.

The other difference was one of color. The hilltops around showed brilliantly green in the light of the early morning sun, but what there was to see of Resthaven was black-brown, and milling on it were black-brown creatures. Pedigree Gloucester Old

Spots they might be, but no one would have known, for the herd had rooted and routed over every square inch, looking for something—anything—to eat, and they were plastered with dirt.

As the Pigman had said, there was no problem about drinking, for millions and millions of gallons of water flowed by them. It was food they were thinking about, and the first thing they had done was to graze off every blade of grass and gobble up every dock and nettle, even every thistle; every leaf and shoot they could reach through the boundary pig wire they had torn off, and where a hedgerow tree was close enough, they had chewed its bark. Then they had turned up the whole top triangle of the field and ferreted out the roots of every blade of grass, every patch of clover, every weed. Anything they came across went down them—worms, slugs, beetles, even some families of field mice, babies and all, and of all the hundreds of ant heaps that had dotted the upper slopes of Resthaven only one remained, and on it, yellow against the black-brown background, the Pigman still sat, head hanging, shoulders bowed, stomach rumbling with hunger.

Mrs. Barleylove and Daggie were just as black and filthy as the rest, for they, too, had been rooting everywhere for food. Only Felicity was spotlessly clean, not a black or a white feather out of place, for she, of course, had flown onto the flood for a thorough bath. She stood now on Mrs. Barleylove's broad back, to be out of the way of the pushing, shoving, squealing multitude of earth-covered pigs, and spoke into the big droopy ear, softly so as not to be overheard.

"Look, madam," she said. "We've got to do something—you know that as well as I do. This crowd's so hungry they're eating anything now. Let one little piglet get trodden on and they'll gobble him up. And then they'll start on one another. I'm right, don't you think?"

Mrs. Barleylove shuddered. She knew how every

pig worships food, and she was well aware, though she didn't know the word, that pigs are omnivorous, eating everything that is remotely edible. She remembered stories that her mother had told her of swill-feeding in the old days, when rats and sometimes cats would fall into the swill tubs and get cooked: the pigs would chomp them up quite happily, her mother had said.

" 'Course you're right, my dear," she said quietly. "We've got to get help. We've got to get food. But how? It doesn't look like the servant can swim or he'd have gone. And your going wouldn't do much good, if you'll excuse me; people wouldn't connect a Muscovy duck with a herd of pigs. The only one that can swim, after all, is . . ." She stopped, and her mouth fell open.

"Oh, no!" cried Mrs. Barleylove. "Oh, no! Not him!"

"It's got to be your Daggie," said Felicity. "If nobody goes, and no one comes to find you all, and the floods don't go down for a week, say, all hell will break loose here."

"But he may be drowned!" wailed Mrs. Barleylove.

"I don't think so," said Felicity, "though I admit it's a possibility. As against the probability," she said very slowly and clearly, "that if he stays here, he'll be . . . eaten."

There was a small silence between them, in the middle of the uproar of empty-bellied pigs.

"All right," grunted Mrs. Barleylove at last. "If he's willing, bless his little heart," and she blinked her white-lashed eyes very quickly. "But you'll go with him, dear, won't you? Please?"

"Of course," said Felicity. "Try not to worry, madam. I'm sure it'll all have a happy ending. If we can find some other servants like Duckman—er, Pigman, I mean—somewhere downstream, they'll see Daggie's spots and they'll know where he's from. After all, there's only this one herd of Gloucester Old Spots in the district, isn't there?"

"Far as I know," said Mrs. Barleylove.

"Well, then," said the duck, "they'll know something's wrong. And they'll get food here somehow, by boat or helicopter."

The sow had no notion what a helicopter was, but she had a lot of faith in Felicity, and she called loudly to her son.

Daggie came running. He was very hungry, for his mother's milk had dried up now, and he had been pushed and shoved away from anything that looked like food by his stronger brethren. But his eyes were bright and his courage was high, and as soon as he heard about the plan, he was wild to go.

Felicity flew down to the water's edge, and Mrs. Barleylove followed, barging her way through the press of pigs with Daggie at her heels. "Coming through! Coming through!" she shouted, and the other sows, hearing her voice, pushed forward to see what was happening.

They were all asking questions at once when sharp squeals from above made them look around. They saw the Squire come rolling down toward them, his tusks showing white in his muddy face as he tossed pig after pig out of his way.

"What's going on?" he asked in his deep voice when he reached the sows. "Mrs. Barleylove, dear lady, what's going on?"

"It's my son, Squire," replied Mrs. Barleylove proudly. "He's going for help. He's going to swim for help, to find someone to bring us food."

Those nearest to her heard her words, and as the news spread the herd fell silent, and every head was turned to listen.

"Your son?" said the Squire loudly. "Your son?"

"Our son, Squire," said Mrs. Barleylove softly, feeling her white parts turn pink, and thankful for the mud that hid them.

"That's better," said the Squire, and turning to the little piglet, he looked curiously at him. Little shrimp, he thought, he's not much bigger than a rat. And those front feet . . .

He spoke quietly now, so that the pigs at the edge of the crowd raised their heads to hear better as the great boar looked down at the little dag.

"So you're Daggie Dogfoot," said the Squire.

"Yes, sir," said Daggie politely.

"And you're going for help?"

"Yes, sir."

"Current's strong, you know. Water's deep. Understand you can—er—swim pretty well, but it'll be dangerous."

"Oh, I'll be all right," said Daggie. "Thank you, Father," he added daringly. The boar cleared his throat as though there were some kind of lump in it.

"Well, good luck, my son," he said in a loud, strained voice. "By Saint Anthony, I wish you the very best of good luck."

And the mob of pigs echoed him. "Good luck! Good luck!" they cried, and the Pigman got up off his ant heap at the noise and lumbered down to find out what it was all about.

He was just in time to see Daggie walk out into the shallows, the mud on him dissolving as the current began to wash him clean. Soon he was swimming, once again a white piglet with black spots, and then he was in midstream and the full force of the floodwater took him and whirled him away.

But every pig could see how beautifully he swam, and most of them could hear his farewell cry. One of them stood alone, belly-deep in the shallows, while a great tear ran down each of her fat cheeks and plopped into the stream. Come back safely, my Daggie, said Mrs. Barleylove to herself.

Just then Felicity came flying back, low over the heads of the herd. The Pigman had taken off his hat, the better to scratch his head in his utter bewilderment at the sight of a swimming pig, and Felicity dived down, caught it in her clawed feet and tore it from him.

"I'll take this with me," she shouted to Mrs. Barleylove, as she wheeled to follow Daggie. "Maybe someone will know who this belongs to," and she flew rapidly away, the hat dangling below her, while the Pigman danced in anger.

"Dratyer!" he cried, and "Dangyer!" and "Blast-yer!" shaking his huge fist at the two fast-disappearing figures.

"Stupid, ignorant duck!" he shouted. "You and that horrible little dag, you make a fine pair. Never be no use to no one, not neither of you, nohow!"

And as the pigs ran to the topmost part of Rest-haven, they caught a final glimpse of Daggie Dog-foot, far down on the flood. They could see Felicity for a little longer as she flew low, directly above the swimmer. And then there was nothing to be seen but a great waste of waters.

13

Man on a Raft

Jumping around in anger had awakened the Pigman's brain from the daze of hopelessness into
which it had fallen, and he began to think what he
could do about the situation. It occurred to him, as it
had to the duck much earlier, that there would be
trouble with a capital T if the pigs remained unfed.
His shed, he knew, was gone, and help, if it ever
came, might be a long time arriving. After much
head scratching, a simple idea came to him. Resthaven, after all, was only one side of the little conical
hill on which they were marooned, so that there
must be grass and bushes and trees on the other
side. All he had to do was to take down the pig wire

that confined his herd, and then they could find something to keep them going.

To do this was not easy, since the fence had been well made in the first place, tightly stretched, and nailed to posts. Wire cutters would have done the job in a minute, but, of course, he had none with him. As he stood and looked at the fence, the Squire rolled up and stood beside him. They conversed in their separate languages.

"If only you had the brains, old fellow," said the Pigman, "you'd get your head under the wire and lift it up."

"If you had any sense at all, Pigman," said the Squire, "you'd use that branch that's lying there as a lever to get the bottom of this wire up far enough for me to put my head under it."

"If I had something for a lever," said the Pigman, "I might be able to lift the bottom of it a little. Then perhaps this old boar would see what I'm getting at."

"Man's a fool," said the Squire.

"Oh, there's a branch," said the Pigman. "That might do."

"At last," said the Squire with a sigh, as the Pigman slid the branch under the lowest-but-one strand of the pig wire, stuck the far end into the ground beyond, and began to heave upward. With great effort he managed to lift the bottom strand six inches above the ground.

"Ladies!" shouted the Squire. "I want you all on parade, please. Chop-chop!" And when the nine sows came galloping up, he said more quietly, "Spread out, please. Four on one side of me, five on the other. Snouts down. Wait for my word." And from the corner of his mouth he snarled at the servant, "Come on, Man!"

Almost as though he could understand, the Pigman redoubled his efforts. The bottom of the wire rose a fraction higher, the boar got his head under the lowest strand, then the sow on either side of him, and so on, until all ten heads were under and all ten great bodies tensed.

"Ready! Steady! Heave!" shouted the Squire, and with a twanging, tearing noise a twenty-foot stretch of pig wire rose up, up, up, till the retaining fence posts popped out of the ground.

"Forward!" bawled the Squire, and before the advancing weight of more than four thousand pounds of pig, the fence burst like a rotten tennis net, and the rest of the herd poured through. They went around the back of the hill, snatching at the fresh grass like mad things, and the Pigman was left alone.

The sight of his animals eating again reminded

him painfully of how empty his own stomach was. If only I had a boat, he thought, and he strained his little piggy eyes upstream as though wishing would make one appear. He did not see one, of course, but he did see something—two things, in fact. They were about ten feet apart, halfway between him and his drowned buildings, and he suddenly realized that they were the tops of the gateposts at the entrance to Resthaven.

Gateposts, he thought. Water must have gone down a little; couldn't see them before. Gateposts, he thought. There's a gate between 'em. Gate, he thought. Made of wood. Wood, he thought. Floats. Floats, he thought. Like a boat—well, like a raft.

He went down to the water's edge and began to wade back toward the gateposts. The current was strong, but the Pigman was powerful, and he fought his way along, deeper and deeper as he went down the slope. He was shoulder deep when at last he stood between the posts and, feeling underwater, found the gate.

Now was the moment of decision for the Pigman. As Mrs. Barleylove had guessed, he could not swim. Moreover, he was afraid of the water. As a child, he had once been taken to the beach on a school outing, but nothing would persuade him to go beyond the ripples. What he was doing now was, for him, an act of great bravery. But more was needed. In order to grip the heavy gate and clear it from the gatepost, he would need, at this depth, to put his head under the dreaded water!

And if he lifted it free, would it bear him? And if it bore him, where to? To food and shelter and help? Or out to the endless ocean? Desperate men do desperate things, and the Pigman closed his eyes, settled his feet firmly, and took a good grip and a deep, deep breath.

There followed a scene that would have seemed pure comedy if there had been a human watcher unaware of the underlying drama, but, for the Pigman, it could easily have been one of tragedy.

To begin with, the hinges were jammed on the gateposts, and it took three increasingly breathless dips below the surface before his utmost efforts could lift the gate free. And when it was free, the current immediately dragged it away, so that the Pigman had to make a wild, belly-flopping leap at it as it went. He caught the back end of it, whereupon it tipped up like a live thing, threatening to throw him off into deeper water. Somehow, gasping, spluttering, panic-stricken, he managed to scramble farther onto it, expecting all the time that it would submerge beneath him.

But it bore him, though the weight of the heavy man and his waterlogged clothes pushed it below the surface, so that he would have appeared, if there had been a watcher, to be floating motionless on the flood, like a bright yellow hippopotamus.

This was what he looked like to the first eyes that did see him. Most of the herd were on the reverse side of the hill, rooting and tearing at anything they could find, but the Squire and Mrs. Barleylove had not moved far from the break in the fence, and it was they who witnessed the Pigman's progress.

"By Saint Anthony!" the Squire burst out. "It's the servant! Seems to be lying on top of the water. Extraordinary! Fellow can't be as stupid as I thought."

Mrs. Barleylove watched as the current bore the Pigman steadily away. Daggie, she thought, where are you, darling?

"I'll be on the lookout," said the Squire, reading her thoughts, "when the level drops a bit more, so I can see the line of the hedges or fences. Should be easy to bust 'em."

"Easier with two, Squire," said Mrs. Barleylove.

Champion Imperial Challenger III of Ploughbarrow raised his heavy head and gazed at this wife of his with approval and affection. "Couldn't wish for a better partner," he said. "And try not to worry too much about the boy. We'll find him. You'll see."

14

On the Dam

Not long after Daggie and Felicity had disappeared
from the sight of the watching herd, the course of the
flood took a turn in a new direction, and the course
of their fortunes took a turn for the better. A mile or
so from Resthaven the old brook had rounded the
foot of a high spur, plunged, southwest and sea-
wards, into quite a deep, steep valley and, though
now swollen to many times its usual width, was
nonetheless narrower at this point than the broad
waters on which Daggie had begun his swim. Conse-
quently the speed of the current increased dramati-
cally, so that Felicity needed to fly at her fastest to
keep up with the swimmer.

Daggie, of course, was too excited to be frightened. "Wheeeeeee!" he yelled as the racing water swept him along, but the Muscovy, ten feet above him, suddenly saw trouble ahead.

Something was blocking the way—a kind of rough dam, it seemed, though Felicity could not see what it was made of. But she could see that the rushing flood parted before it, swerved away to either side, and fell from sight in a boiling swirl. Felicity knew something about waterfalls and the terrible currents beneath them, and she instantly realized the awful danger Daggie would be in if he was swept over the falls.

Flying her hardest, she dropped low over the piglet, the strings of the yellow rain hat held tight in her claws, the rest of it hanging low.

"Grab it in your teeth, Daggie!" she shouted. "Quick! Don't argue!"

As soon as she felt his weight, she turned and faced upstream, beating her wings with all her strength. Try as she might, she could still feel herself being dragged backward, but at least she was cutting down Daggie's breakneck speed and keeping him dead center.

When a hasty glance over her shoulder told her the moment was ripe, she turned and dropped down onto a branch that stuck out at water level. She walked backward along the branch, pulled as hard as she could, and landed Daggie as an angler lands a fish. They were safe on the dam, and they could hear the thunder of falling water behind and below them.

Its purpose served, the yellow rain hat slipped over the falls on the start of a journey that was to bring help, for someone spotted it far downstream and fished it out, and inside it they could still make out the Pigman's name and address written in his horrible scrawl.

"Gosh, that thing tasted nasty," panted Daggie, wrinkling his snout. "What was that all about, Felicity?"

Felicity looked at him and made her quot-quot-quotting noise.

"Oh, nothing," she said. "I just thought we'd have a breather. Let's look around."

Curiously, perhaps because he was so breathless, sight was the last of Daggie's five senses to send messages to his brain. With the roar of the falls in his ears and the sour taste of oilskin in his mouth, the next thing he realized, through his sensitive forefeet, was that the bark of the big branch on which he was standing was familiarly rough, as though he had met, not just this *kind* of tree, but this *particular* tree before. Then suddenly, lifting his snout to the wind, he smelled food! And not just food, but pig food! And not just pig food somewhere miles away, but pig food near, very near, here, right

on this jumble of objects in the middle of the stream!
Then at last—and all this happened in a matter of
seconds—he used his eyes. What he suddenly saw
excited him so much that he nearly lost his perch
and fell into the water again.

"Look, Felicity!" he shouted. "Look—behind
you!"

And there, jammed among the branches, was the
shed. It was still upright, its door still hung open,

and out of the door came the wonderful smells. Like shipwrecked mariners stumbling on treasure, they scrambled toward it.

Inside, the bins of barley meal and middlings and flaked corn still stood, their wooden lids tightly shut and far too heavy to be lifted by piglet or duck. But that did not matter, for on the floor were sacks of pignuts that had fallen as the shed had tossed on the flood. Some of these had broken open so that part of the floor was covered with a rich dark brown carpet of nuts, which Daggie pounced on. Some of this carpet had been wet into a beautiful mush by water seeping through the floorboards, so that Felicity could suck up a kind of delicious pignut porridge. For a long time there was nothing to be heard in the shed but the sounds of eating.

Felicity stopped eating first, because her crop was full. She went out to the edge of the dam for a drink. When her thirst was satisfied, she flew around to look at the far side of the obstruction. She found, as she had suspected, that the jam of timber had caused a wicked waterfall down which Daggie would surely have plunged to a horrible death.

When she came back into the shed, he was still eating. At last he staggered out and picked his way to the water and drank deeply. When he returned, he let out a huge belch, followed by a long sigh of contentment, flopped on his side on the floor, and fell fast asleep, his little spotted balloon of a tummy rising and falling. Not a bad idea, thought the Muscovy, closing her eyes.

An hour or so later Daggie woke suddenly with a shout of "Mommy!" A series of muddled dreams had turned into a nightmare, something to do with his babyhood, and sure enough, the very first thing he focused on was the hardwood club, still hanging on its rusty nail. Then he saw the kind face of his friend Felicity looking down at him from the top of a bin, and he remembered what had happened. Looking out the doorway, he saw a big branch that stuck up in the air, and on the branch were familiar crinkly-edged leaves, and among the leaves were some acorns.

"It's the oak, isn't it, Felicity?" he said. "It's the old oak from Resthaven."

"Yes," said the duck. "It jammed across this narrow place, against some rocks probably, and then caught everything else that came down, including, thank goodness, this shed."

"Gosh, yes," said Daggie. "What luck! What super grub. I feel like a new piglet."

"You look like a new piglet," said Felicity. "Your mother wouldn't recognize you."

Daggie's mood changed instantly. "Mommy!" he cried, jumping to his feet. "Oh, Mommy! Oh, how selfish I am! Here I am, making a pig of myself, and all the time Mommy's hungry, starving perhaps. And Father. And my aunts. And my brothers and sisters. And all the others. Oh, what a selfish pig I am!"

"Don't be silly," said Felicity shortly. "It's only sensible that as we've been lucky enough to find all this food, we should eat our fill. We must keep up our strength, you know. There's an awful lot to do."

"Yes, I suppose so," said Daggie, a little less miserably. "But what can we do? How can we get this food back to the others? We can't carry it."

"I don't know," said Felicity. "I honestly don't know. But I have a feeling that something will turn up." And she began to preen herself and to rearrange her feathers, while Daggie lay down again on his distended stomach and gazed out the doorway.

And as he gazed, something did turn up. At first Daggie could not see clearly what it was, for the sun was in his eyes. All he noticed was a yellowish lump in the distance, coming down toward them—a dead tree perhaps, he thought. But as it came nearer, he could see that it was not vegetable but animal, that it was not dead but alive, for it had a staring white face and wide flaring nostrils, and its teeth were bared in a grin of fear, while its tongue licked nervously over its thick lips. Its body, he could now see, was bright yellow, and it seemed to ride effortlessly on the water.

"Felicity!" yelled Daggie in an agony of terror. "A monster! A monster! He's coming straight at us!"

Felicity waddled to the door.

"I hope he is," she said. "We need him. It's Duckman."

15

Breakfast and Bed

The Pigman, low in the water, did not realize the danger ahead. Even if he had, it is doubtful that he could have done much about it, so paralyzed was he with terror. All he was concerned with was hanging onto his gate like grim death. This, in fact, was what saved him, for when the current took hold and whirled him off to one side of the dam and over the falls, he held tight; if he had let go then, he would probably have been sucked under by the down currents in the pool below, and drowned.

Felicity, flying toward the other side of the dam, saw the man and his raft plunge down beneath the boiling surface. But then the heavy wooden gate rose **again**, its rider still clinging to it, water cascading off the soaking yellow oilskins. Once he's clear of the pool down there and out in midstream again, he'll be gone, with nothing to stop him between here and the sea, thought Felicity. But at that moment a freakish current dragged the gate back toward the dam, toward a point where a strong branch 'of the old oak stuck out invitingly.

"If only he'd let go of the gate and grab that branch," shouted the Muscovy over the noise of the falls to Daggie, who was standing above, watching. "Otherwise he'll be gone in a minute."

Inspiration came to Daggie.

"Scratch his hands, Felicity," he yelled. "Fly down and scratch his hands. That'll make him let go!"

As the piglet looked on, Felicity flew down, pitched on the end of the gate, and deliberately dragged her sharp claws across the backs of the Pigman's tightly gripping hands. Then everything happened at once. The Pigman loosened his hold with a yell of pain and anger and grabbed frantically at the branch. The gate shot from under him, caught the force of the stream again, and sailed steadily away. The duck flew back onto the dam and perched beside Daggie.

Side by side, the friends watched anxiously as the

Pigman struggled to pull himself along the branch to safety. His clothes were soaked, his boots full of water, his tired limbs cramped, his hungry body chilled. But he was strong and he was desperate, and at last, somehow, he scrambled onto the dam.

For a while he lay in the tangle of timber, gasping for breath. When at last he sat up and looked around, he saw the two watchers, and some color came back into his wet white face.

"Dratyer!" he cried, shaking his bleeding fists at them, and "Dangyer!" and "Blastyer!"

Then suddenly he lurched to his feet. His mouth, open from the last shout, gaped wider still, his piggy eyes glinted, and in a kind of mad blundering stumble he began to clamber over the mess of timber in the direction of the two animals.

Hurriedly the stupid, ignorant duck and the horrible little dag moved out of the way, but they soon realized the reason for the servant's excitement. Pigman had seen the back of the shed.

Above everything else, the Pigman was hungry, excruciatingly, ravenously hungry. For most of the thirty-odd hours that had passed since he ran from this shed in the face of the approaching flood, he had thought of food in general, and in particular of some sandwiches left in the pocket of his old apron (the very pocket that had once carried Daggie), which hung from a second rusty nail beside the hardwood club. They were ham sandwiches, his favorite, and the spittle ran down over his three chins as he fought his way to the door.

He clambered in, and there was the apron. He plunged his huge hand into the pocket, and there were the sandwiches. He tore off the paper in which they were wrapped and crammed them into his mouth. By the time Daggie and Felicity had summoned up courage to peep around the door, the sandwiches were gone, for there had been only two, meant for a mid-morning snack. As they watched, the Pigman broke open a sack of pignuts, picked out a handful, and began to chew them. A cautious look came over his face, then something like a smile, and then he sat down and began to stuff himself.

"Gosh, he must be full," said Daggie after a while. "What do you think he'll do next?"

"Don't know what to think," said Felicity. "First he comes floating down the river like a duck . . ."

". . . and then he makes a pig of himself!" laughed Daggie. "Extraordinary fellow, doncherknow!" he said in a passable imitation of his father, and they both giggled in a chorus of little grunts and quot-quot-quotting noises.

The Pigman had, in fact, decided what to do next. He had never had a deep thought in his whole life, but when certain simple ideas occurred to him, he acted on them without further ado.

At the moment his stomach was full, but the rest of his body was wet and cold and tired. His brain therefore received three messages. Get dry. Get warm. Get sleep.

The two heads looking around the door saw the Pigman move slowly into action. First he took off his yellow oilskins and hung them on a third rusty nail beside the apron and the hardwood club. Then he opened the three big wooden meal bins one after the other and looked into each long and earnestly, scratching his head like mad. At the last one, the flaked corn bin, he took off his rubber boots, emptied the water out of them onto the floor, and then solemnly filled them full of the crackly golden stuff.

Next he went to the middlings bin. He took off his trousers, his pullover, his shirt, and his socks, and carefully buried them all deep in the brown sawdusty stuff.

Then the Pigman, clothed only in gray woolen underwear, went to the barley bin. Laboriously, with much grunting, he climbed into the bin and began to work himself down into the thick white powdery stuff like some giant lugworm burying itself in soft sand. When he was waist deep in it, he reached up to a shelf above for a bundle of old copies of *The Pig Breeder's Gazette*. He wriggled on down till he was shoulder deep. Then he slipped the magazines under his head, plunged his arms under the barley blanket, and lay back with a sigh.

"By Saint Anthony," said Daggie mischievously as the Pigman closed his eyes, "fellow's actually going to sleep," and they both burst into another fit of giggles.

16
Dreams

'Water's actually going down a bit," said the Squire. "Take a look at those young porkers over there, Mrs. Barleylove. They're grazing grass that was underwater a few hours ago."

By now the hungry herd had eaten everything growing on the little hill of which Resthaven formed a part so that the whole of it was now a black-brown hump. But at its edges a fresh green rim kept appearing as the flood level gradually dropped, and as fast as it appeared, the herd ate it. The vegetable matter kept them going, but such a diet was rather like humans living on nothing but soggy lettuce, and they longed for solid substantial food.

"Couldn't we try to get downstream now, Squire?" asked Mrs. Barleylove. Her belly ached for a square meal, and her heart ached for Daggie. The Squire heard the note of pleading in her voice and nodded his heavy head.

"Not long now, dear lady," he said. "I don't think much of either of us as swimmers, doncherknow, so we mustn't go beyond our depth. But you can see the line of the willows at the edge of the brook pretty clearly now. And the tops of some fences."

He thought for a moment. Then he gave his deep coughing grunt and shouted, "Ladies! This way, please. Chop-chop!"

When the other eight sows had joined Mrs. Barleylove and all were standing around him in a respectful circle, he addressed them thus:

"Listen carefully, please, ladies. Don't want to have to repeat myself. Now, it doesn't look as though help were coming. On the other trotter, water's dropping. Not enough yet to get the youngsters downstream, but Mrs. Barleylove and I are going to take a little stroll and see what we can find." He paused. "Any objections?" he barked, but the sows noticed the fierceness of his look and said nothing.

"All right then," said the Squire. "Look after the herd. And, ladies, one last thing. Do not attempt to follow us." And he waded off, breast-deep, Mrs. Barleylove in his wake.

Back at the shed, everyone was now asleep and dreaming. Felicity dreamed her usual simple happy kind of dream, all peace and warm sunlight and dancing water.

The Pigman's dream was more complex, and, like his waking thoughts, concerned food. A dream smell of roast suckling pig ran up his flaring nostrils, and he stirred restlessly in the barley meal bin, his white-lashed eyelids fluttering.

Daggie was having a nightmare. He lay in a pool of sunlight by the door, but in his mind he was back in Resthaven, before the flood, playing King of the Castle, jumping on Mommy's big stomach. Outside the shed the real sun disappeared behind a cloud bank, and the pool of sunlight was no more. And in his dream, too, the day turned gray, and his mommy vanished, and something horrible was coming toward him, something huge and fat and white.

The Pigman had settled so low in the barley meal that eventually he snored some of the floury stuff right up his nose. He woke up and rubbed his face with his mealy hands, so that he was white from top to toe. His brain received a message: I am thirsty. He lifted himself out of the bin.

Then everything happened at once. Daggie woke and squealed with terror as his nightmare became reality. Felicity woke, and thinking her friend to be in danger, flew at the Pigman's head. The Pigman put up his hands to ward her off, tripped as the piglet dashed between his legs, stubbed his toe in the doorway, caught his foot in a branch outside, and like a great tree falling, crashed into the water and sank below the surface.

As Daggie and Felicity watched, horrified, they saw on the far bank two great spotted figures galloping down toward the pool, and they heard in the distance a strange clattering noise.

The Pigman's head broke through the surface of the water. "Heeeelp!" he roared. "Heee-gurgle-glug!" and down he went again.

17

The Big Strange Bird

Back at Resthaven, things were looking up. To be more exact, pigs were looking up, at a big strange bird in the sky.

They had heard the bird before they had seen it, for it had a loud rattling voice, and they raised their heads and watched it appear over the eastern hills. It flew down the valley toward them, pausing over the mill with its ruined pond, and again over the farm buildings, now almost empty of water. Its glassy eyes twinkled in the bright sunlight, and its wings whirled above its body at great speed.

Suddenly it saw the herd in Resthaven, and it darted sideways toward the pigs and hovered above the little hill like some huge hawk, so low that they could feel the terrible wind of it. None of the pigs had ever seen a helicopter before, and they galloped around in panic. But the bird came no lower, so they gathered in a nervous huddle and watched as a hole appeared in its side and a brown object fell out of it.

"It's layin' eggs on us!" shouted Mrs. Grubguzzle in alarm, but before the words were out of her mouth, the brown object hit the ground and burst open. A familiar smell came wafting to the snouts of the herd, growing stronger by the minute as two, four, eight more sacks of pignuts were tipped from the door of the helicopter. Then it turned and slid away westward down the line of the brook.

When the helicopter reached the dam, the strangest scene met its glassy eyes. If it had really been a bird, it would have had the tallest of tall stories to tell to its children. As it was, of course, there were three men in it: the pilot, the observer, and the winchman. And in later years, when they had children of their own, old enough for storytelling, they all told the same tale to their goggle-eyed families.

It was during the Great Summer Flood, they said, when people and animals in that part of the country had been cut off from supplies. Alerted by the discovery of the yellow rain hat, they had been sent to an isolated pig farm and had found a herd of pigs and dropped food for them. Then—"And you'll

never believe this," each said—they had come to a
place where a big jumble of uprooted trees and other
rubbish, including what looked like a shed, had
dammed the stream and formed a big pool.

On one side of this pool stood two great spotted
pigs. And flying above the pool was a black-and-
white duck. And in the middle of the pool was a
man—a huge fat man from what they could see of
him—struggling madly in the water; they could
hear nothing because of the noise of their helicopter,
but they could see his mouth open in a shout for help
before he went down again.

Then—"It's true, I promise you," each said—a
little spotty piglet—"odd-looking thing with a head
too big for its body and funny feet"—dived off the
dam into the pool, swam—"yes, *swam*"—across it
at tremendous speed, and seemed to say something
to the two big pigs. They in turn put their heads
down and tipped a piece of wood into the pool—"it
was a fence post"—and the piglet lined it up so the
sharp end was pointing at the struggling man
—"Cross my heart." Then it swam around and
pressed its snout to the blunt end—"Scout's honor."
The duck landed on top of the stake and flapped its
wings like mad—"Honest to goodness"—and the
piglet swam like crazy, and the stake went whizzing
across the pool like a torpedo, and they got to the
man just as he was going down for the third time,

and he managed to grab the stake and hang onto it, and so the duck and the amazing swimming piglet saved his life.

"But is all that really true, Dad?" asked each of the families.

"Of course it is," said each father.

And, of course, it was.

"Saved my life, saved my life," babbled the Pigman as he lay on the floor of the clattering helicopter. "And to think I called 'em stupid and ignorant and horrible! And now see what they've done for me. I'll make it up to 'em, I'll make it up to 'em. You see if I don't."

"Yes, yes, old man," said the helicopter pilot

soothingly. "Just you relax and don't worry. We'll get you to the hospital right away."

"Hospital?" said the Pigman loudly, struggling to his wet feet. "I don't want to go to no hospital. You get me back to the farm. I've got a job to do. I've got to get everything ready for 'em. When they come home."

18
Missing

By evening the herd was comfortably full of food and the Pigman once again ragingly hungry. He stood beside the helicopter, which had landed in the yard, and stared at the concrete foundation where the shed had stood. He was shocked and soaked, and his sluggish brain was hardly working at all. What thoughts he had were all of eating. But not pig meat, not ever again, he said slowly to himself. Not ever again. Nor duck. Not after what they did for me. Not nohow.

And almost as though he were a mind reader, the helicopter pilot said, "You must be pretty hungry, old buddy. I mean, we had a good breakfast of bacon

and eggs"—the Pigman shuddered—"but you probably haven't eaten for days. Have my sandwiches.
They're Spam."

"I couldn't," said the Pigman in a low voice, and,
thinking that he was too embarrassed to accept their
hospitality, the observer said in a friendly tone,
"Well, I can offer you something better than Spam,
old buddy. Have mine. They're duck paste."

"Oh, I couldn't," said the Pigman, more miserable
than ever.

"You're welcome to mine," said the winchman,
holding out some large foil-wrapped sandwiches,
"but they're nothing special."

"What are they?" asked the Pigman in a tremu-
lous voice.

"Peanut butter," said the winchman, and then
drew back in surprise as, with a great grunt of
delight, the Pigman snatched the sandwiches from
his hands, tore off the wrapping, and stuffed the
whole wad in his mouth.

The helicopter crew watched silently as the Pigman chomped and chewed with his strong yellow
tusks, his big nostrils flaring, his little eyes shut tight
in ecstasy.

No wonder he's fat as a pig, thought the pilot.

Talk about greedy as a pig, thought the observer.

He sure looks like a pig, thought the winchman, as
with a last snort of pleasure the Pigman finished the

sandwiches and ran his tongue over his lips in search of crumbs.

And almost as though he were reading the crew's thoughts, the Pigman suddenly shouted, "Pigs!"

"What do you mean?" cried the pilot as all three of them jumped back nervously.

"Pigs. My pigs. Out there." The Pigman gestured toward Resthaven. "They must be starved. Got to get grub to 'em. Got to get my shed back somehow."

They explained to him that they had dropped some food. And then the pilot said, "That hut thing we sighted—where we pulled you out of the water —is that your shed?"

"That's her," said the Pigman.

"How did it get there?"

"She floated."

"Well," said the pilot, "how about our towing the thing back for you? If it floated down, it might float back. It's no use to you down there."

So they left the Pigman with dry clothing and lifted away downstream. On their way to the dam, they passed the black-and-white duck flying toward the farm.

Felicity landed on her perch in the alder tree and looked around. In the distance she could see the herd in Resthaven. They were lying in the sunshine, apparently contented. Beyond them, she could just make out the figures of the Squire and Mrs. Barleylove splashing homeward. The Pigman was hard at work sweeping the last of the water from the sties and bringing dry bedding straw from the top of the barn, where the flood had not reached it. He was a picture in navy blue overalls and boots. Everything's returning to normal, Felicity thought to herself. Except for the shed, but that's asking a bit much.

But it wasn't, for before long she heard the rattly voice of the big strange bird, and there beneath and behind it was the shed, stately as a galleon, coming slowly upstream on the end of a long towrope.

At the dam both winchman and observer had gone down the cable while the pilot hovered, and had fastened a rope under the shed as though tying a giant parcel. Now, close by Felicity's alder tree, the winchman released the towrope, refastened the cable to the top of the parcel, and raised his hand.

Gradually the shed rose out of the stream, timbers creaking, door swinging, sailed over the buildings, and was lowered, gently, exactly, onto its foundation. The rope was released and drawn up, and once again the helicopter dropped down into the yard.

"O.K.?" shouted the pilot to the Pigman. "All right now? All your pigs back?"

"I'll just check," yelled the Pigman, and he walked out into Resthaven.

Five minutes later he was running back, his big

face white and his fat cheeks wobbling.

"My dag! My little dag!" he shouted. "He hasn't come home!"

"Dag?" cried the pilot.

"Yes! The one who saved my life!" roared the Pigman, and tears came out of his piggy eyes and ran down his cheeks and over the hills and valleys of his three chins.

"Oh, is that what he's called?" yelled the pilot. "Well, don't worry, old man. We'll fly back and see where he is. He's probably swimming home." And away they went downstream again.

19

An Awful Shock

When the Squire and Mrs. Barleylove had started home from the dam, they had given Daggie permission to go on ahead of them. They did not believe he could come to any harm on the fast-drying bank. He's a big boy now, and sensible, they said to each other.

But like any adventurous youngster, Daggie decided to do not what he had been told but something much more exciting instead.

"Let them go home by land," he said loudly as soon as he was out of earshot. "I'm a swimming pig, and I'm going to swim home."

He hid himself until he saw the shed sailing by,

and until his mother and father had passed him and disappeared. Then he slipped into the water.

The current was still fairly strong, but he was confident he could swim against it. Still, he thought he would start in a quiet place, a deep inlet that was out of the main run of water. He glided out from the bank, but instead of going straight into his usual racing crawl, he decided to splash and play. He put his head under and found himself staring into a pair of cold, hard eyes, set behind narrow wolf jaws, and backed by a long barred body.

Before he could move, there was an explosion in the depths beneath him. He felt a violent blow that almost lifted him out of the water, and the pike clamped its jaws on the end of his snout.

In an agony of fear Daggie pulled back with all his strength, thrashing and flailing in the water as he tried to get free. But the pike was bigger than he, and stronger than he, and its cruel teeth were tight in his tender nose, and he could not breathe. Gradually he grew weaker, and gradually the fierce fish pulled him deeper, and his mind began to spin, and a whole series of faces flashed across it, all in a split second: his mommy's face, and the faces of his father the Squire, and his kind aunts, and the servant, and Felicity. And before his whirling senses became a blank, black emptiness, there sounded in his ear a thin, hard cry.

"I-zaak!" it seemed to say. "I-zaak!"

When Daggie Dogfoot came to, there was still a face in front of him,. But this time it was a real face, a live face, a round whiskery face wearing a look of deep anxiety. And out of it came a worried voice.

"Old pig! Old pig!" the voice said. "You're all right, aren't you? You're all right? Now don't say you're not, 'cause you are."

Daggie looked around him and found that he was lying in the grass on the bank of the brook. He spit out a lot of water and lay panting, his whole body shaking with shock.

"Ike!" he croaked. "Oh, Ike! What happened? What was it? Oh, my nose! And the back of my neck!"

"What happened, old pig," said Ike, "was that you came pretty close to being drowned and eaten, and don't say you didn't, 'cause you did. Your nose is sore because you've had a couple of dozen razor-sharp teeth stuck in it, and your neck's sore because I had to haul you out by the scruff."

"But what was it, Ike? What was that dreadful fish?"

"Pike," said Ike. "That was a pike, old pig."

"But it was so big," said Daggie. "I never knew they were as big as that. Felicity never warned me."

"She never knew either, old pig," said Ike. "That's the biggest one ever. Lived in the millpond and got washed out when the sluice gates burst. I've been dying to meet him, and now that I have, *he's* dying!" The otter threw back his head and shook with silent laughter.

Daggie staggered to his feet and looked down into the water. Floating there on its side was the long barred shape of the monster pike of the millpond, the wolf jaws split wide in the gape of agony caused by the otter's death bite. Between the dorsal fin and the tail was a terrible scooped-out gash.

"I broke his back, old pig," said Ike, standing beside the gazing piglet. "And don't say I didn't, 'cause I did. Now I'll pull him out and we'll eat the best of him. I'll be laughing all the way to the bank!"

20

"Not MIGHT, But CAN!"

Daggie was very, very full. He was also, suddenly, very tired, from the strain of all his adventures, and particularly from the shock of the last one. He flopped down on the bank and rolled over into a slight hollow, so that he lay on his back, all four legs stuck up in the air. Immediately he fell into the deepest of deep sleeps.

Minutes passed, and in the bright sunshine bees buzzed and a big fat bluebottle landed neatly on the staring eye of the dead pike.

Suddenly there came a wailing, mewing noise from the blue sky above, and Ike, looking up from the bushes where he was dozing, saw a solitary buzzard circling on wide wings over the sleeping piglet. It had come down from the hills, feeding on the carcasses of drowned sheep.

The otter knew that buzzards were carrion-eating cowards, and he had no fears for Daggie's safety. If his friend did not wake, he thought, he would give it a sudden awful shock. He grinned happily.

The buzzard dropped lower. It could see below what appeared to be a very dead animal, whose belly was blown up like a drum and whose legs stuck out stiffly. Moreover, its nose was caked with dried blood.

The scavenger prepared to land, but at that moment it heard a loud noise in the distance, and a big strange bird with twinkling glassy eyes and wings that whirled above its body came clattering downstream. The buzzard flew away with a cry of alarm, and even the bold Ike slid out of the bushes and into the water, where he lay with only his mask showing and watched. The helicopter checked and the crew peered down.

"There he is!" shouted the observer. "But dead as a doornail by the look of him. Something got the poor little thing. Look at the blood on his snout."

"We'd better pick him up," the pilot said.

"Death of a hero," said the winchman.

"Tell you what," said the pilot. "We can fly him

home in state. After all, he was the one and only swimming pig. Let's give him the grandest possible return to his last resting place."

"On the end of the rescue cable?" said the observer. "So that the mourning multitudes can pay their respects?"

"That's it," said the pilot. "Remember the old saying—'pigs might fly!'" The three young men grinned at each other.

"Well, let's make a good job of it," said the winchman. "I'll go down and strap him on—I can adjust the harness—and then I'll wait here and you can pick me up later when you've delivered him home."

So down went the cable with the winchman, and he fitted the straps around the small spotty body, thinking as he did so that the piglet could not have been dead long; he was so warm. He raised his hand, and the helicopter lifted gently away with Daggie Dogfoot dangling thirty feet below it.

Until that moment—and only Saint Anthony knows how—Daggie had remained in his deepest of sleeps. Through the cries of the buzzard and the rattling of the helicopter and even the harnessing of his body, he had slept on relentlessly. Indeed he had just begun to dream his old dream, of flying with his mother and father through a warm and milky sky, when the tightening of the straps and the rush of air at last wakened him to reality.

Twisting in the harness so that his little legs hung down, he saw below him, fast growing smaller, a man on the ground and an otter in the water, staring up at him. His ears flapped and his tail whirled, and in terrified surprise he kicked like mad with all four legs, his mouth wide open as he squealed with horror. The watchers, two above him, two below, could, of course, not hear his squeal, but they could see that the gallant hero was very much alive. Three of them grinned their relief and pleasure, and the fourth one laughed so much and rocked about so wildly that eventually he sank below the water and swallowed some mouthfuls.

But once he had come to his senses and understood that he was safely anchored to the great bird above, Daggie stopped feeling so panic-stricken and began to look around. Below him, as they gained height for the homeward run, the river became a stream and the stream a trickle. Great trees shrank to the size of thistles, and far below him the swallows flew in ignorance of the miracle above. He opened his mouth wide again, but this time the unheard squeal was of excitement, of happiness, of triumph!

"Pigs might fly!" shouted Daggie. "That's what

Auntie Gobblespud said. Not *might*, but *can*! This pig is flying! So look out, Auntie, look out, Father, look out, Mommy! WHEEEEEEEEEEEEEEE! Here I come!"

21
Home and Dry

Meanwhile, back at the farm, they were indeed looking out, every one of them. The Squire had brought the herd down into the yard and called the roll, and now everyone knew that Daggie was missing, Daggie, who had somehow saved them all by going for help, summoning the great clattering bird, bringing back the servant and his shed. They did not doubt that it was he who had now caused the waters to go down. Probably he could not only swim in them, but could walk on them, too. But would he? Would they ever see him again?

At the distant sound of the approaching helicopter, every head raised. At first they could make out only the machine itself, coming up the line of the brook, a black dot in the eye of the westering sun. But as it drew nearer, they could see below it a small figure and knew themselves to be looking at still another miracle.

And now what rejoicing broke out among the Ploughbarrow herd! How the weaners waltzed and the store pigs sported and the fatteners frolicked!

"We love him!" shouted the eight aunts, shaking their floppy ears. "Isn't he the cleverest ever!"

"Oh, Squire!" cried Mrs. Barleylove. "What's happening? Surely Daggie can't really be flying?"

The great boar looked at her and then up at this amazing son of theirs kicking and flapping and twirling above them.

"By Saint Anthony!" bawled the Squire. "He's doing better than that, my dear. Must be something wrong with that thing, and the boy's towing it in, butchered if he isn't!"

Once above the buildings, the pilot made the helicopter describe a couple of tight circles so that Daggie was whirled around in much larger circles. Felicity flew up to greet him, but he was traveling so fast that she could only catch his squeals of excitement each time he flashed by her on this most marvelous of merry-go-rounds.

Now the helicopter was hovering, directly above the yard, directly above the figure of the Pigman in his new navy overalls, waiting anxiously below. Gradually Daggie's circles grew smaller and slower until at last he hung still. Gently, very gently, the pilot lowered the piglet. Gently, very gently, the piglet touched down. Gently, very gently, the Pigman came forward to release the straps of the harness. To do so, he had to kneel down, and the herd, of course, was duly impressed that at long last the servant was showing a proper degree of respect.

"Hey, you, Pigman. Scratch my back," said Daggie Dogfoot. And the servant, of course, obeyed.

Above them all, the pilot and the observer waved their final farewells before clattering away into the sunset to pick up the winchman and return to their base. And as their racket died away, a shrill, clear whistle pierced the evening air, and a long, low creature with a grinning whiskery face and a battery of sharp white teeth hauled out of the water near Felicity's alder and came to join the pigs.

Now everybody looked at the returned adventurer. And everybody saw his bloody nose, which only one of them knew the reason for. And everybody saw his curious puppy-like forefeet, which some of them knew about. But what everybody saw and everybody knew was that here in front of them was a brave hero, the only dag ever to be taken away and yet come back, who had risked his life on the swollen waters to swim for help. And that help had come, precious food from out of the skies, manna from heaven. Thanks to Daggie Dogfoot, they were all home and dry.

Then the herd turned and moved contentedly away to the familiar comfort of their sties and pens and the pleasant anticipation of a good supper to come. The otter slipped back into the brook and the duck followed him. Only Mrs. Barleylove and the servant still stood by the hero. The Pigman brushed a great hand across his face and sniffed a bit.

"Drat me!" he said softly, and "Dang me!" and "Blast me!" And he, too, turned away and went to prepare the meal.

"Happy, baby?" asked Mrs. Barleylove gently.

"Oh, yes," said Daggie, "but, Mommy, there's just one thing I'd like to do before bedtime. Can I have a swim?"

"Of course," said his mother, and together they walked down through Resthaven to the old pool below the high bank, where the water was almost back to its usual level. The kingfisher sat once again on his perching root, brilliant in the last light of the setting sun, and the rails murmured happily in the reeds. Two bathers were already in the pool.

"Coming in, Daggie?" called Felicity as she twirled and splashed in a shower of golden drops, but he was already gone, running to the top of the slope to prepare for the downhill take-off. "What about you, madam?" the duck asked mischievously. "Going to try it?"

"That'd be a sight to see," said Ike, "and don't say it wouldn't, 'cause it would!" and he opened his mouth very wide and rocked to and fro.

But Mrs. Barleylove wasn't listening. She gave an absentminded grunt and moved up the hill to the spot where the old oak had stood, her eyes on her son.

Daggie Dogfoot turned and began to run downhill at great speed, faster, faster, faster, till at last he leaped out over the high bank of the stream and disappeared from her sight. What clever things her brilliant baby was doing in his favorite element she could not see, but she could hear the joyful squeals and the fluty whistles and the soft quot-quot-quotting noises as he dived and splashed and raced with his friends.

And high above she could hear the cries of the homecoming crows as they circled in the warm air and marveled at the miraculous skills of the amazing swimming pig.

"Caw!" they shouted to one another in awestruck admiration. "Caw! Caw! Caw!"

About the Author

DICK KING-SMITH loves writing, reading, and, of course, pigs. Born in South Gloucestershire, England, he attended Marlborough College, then served with the Grenadier Guards. The realistic view of nature in *Pigs Might Fly* stems from his twenty years of farming. Mr. King-Smith now teaches young children in a village primary school.

Dick King-Smith and his wife have three grown children and four grandchildren, and live in a small cottage in Avon, where they enjoy life in the country.

About the Illustrator

MARY RAYNER created the lively drawings for *Pigs Might Fly* after sketching and photographing Gloucester Old Spot pigs in the children's corner of the London Zoo.

Born in Burma, she now lives in Surrey, England, and has a weekend cottage in Daggie Dogfoot's countryside. Ms. Rayner has written and illustrated several children's books starring pigs.